W9-AXS-785

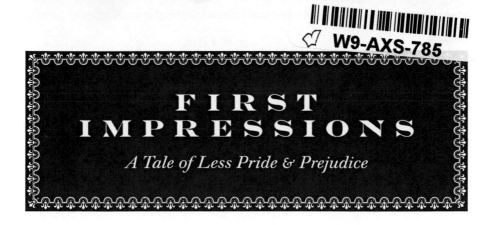

FIRST IMPRESSIONS

A Tale of Less Pride & Prejudice

A L E X A   A D A M S

Outskirts Press, Inc.
Denver, Colorado

First Impressions
A Tale of Less Pride & Prejudice
All Rights Reserved.
Copyright © 2010 Alexa Adams
V1.0

Outskirts Press, Inc.
http://www.outskirtspress.com

ISBN: 978-1-4327-5331-3

Outskirts Press and the "OP" logo are trademarks belonging to Outskirts Press, Inc.

PRINTED IN THE UNITED STATES OF AMERICA

For my Grandmother,
who always wished
that every story would end happily –
preferably by the seaside.

❧

Great thanks to my mother,
my mother-in-law,
and especially my husband for
their unconditional love,
constant support, and excellent
editing skills.

An Apology

It is well acknowledged that every author determined to continue, elaborate on, or simply meddle with Jane Austen's novels must be highly tempted to include a pithy universal truth, in the manner of the lady herself, which establishes the theme of the story. It's almost like a religious ritual, an epic invocation: we call for the great authoress to inspire (and forgive) the games we play with her texts. After all, this is hallowed ground on which we tread. So may I ask you, Miss Austen, to please excuse what I am about to do to your tale of Elizabeth and Darcy? I offer this story in homage to your sense of playfulness, not in some mistaken belief that my pen could ever duplicate yours. You gave each character his or her original essence and to them I will endeavor to be true. I promise to try to not antagonize your delicate sensibilities with the vulgarity of our modern age though I must assume, in spite of my best intentions, that something here will offend. How can it not? The real question is, Jane, do I have your permission to proceed anyway? If only the dead could speak! Perhaps then I would not commit the following atrocity.

Chapter 1

Fitzwilliam Darcy found a quiet corner of the overcrowded assembly hall and breathed an almost silent sigh of relief. From the safety of this retreat he could watch with some degree of composure as his friend, Charles Bingley, smilingly endured the crush of new neighbors from which Darcy had just escaped. Bingley, always deemed universally charming, had somehow managed to maneuver his rather plain dance partner into introducing him to the blonde beauty whom Darcy found to be, unquestionably, the handsomest lady in the room.

Darcy tried to summon a smile in response to his friend's easy sociability but was far too unhinged to succeed in the maneuver. From the moment the Netherfield party made their entrance he could not help but be acutely aware of the familiar buzz that filled the attentive room as Meryton assessed the newcomers. Though he strove to be oblivious as rumor of his income spread through the crowd, the astute observer could clearly perceive the tinge of discomfiture that disfigured his handsome face. No deep observation was required on his part to immediately discern who amongst the strangers surrounding him was privy to the gossip and who remained in ignorance: their overly attentive demeanors told all. He cursed inside. Nothing put him more out of countenance than fawning sycophants and he was displeased to observe that this neighborhood, in which he had unaccountably found himself, had an ample supply. Almost always, except in very elite circles, Darcy felt isolated by his wealth. And when he was amongst his financial equals he felt equally isolated by his values and intelligence as, unfortunately, fortunes were frequently inherited by those of less than stellar abilities. Darcy suffered nearly perpetual discomfort in society but on the evening in question, amongst those he did not know, geniality was proving a particular trial.

Between the songs of the set Bingley sought out his visibly disconcerted friend in the kindhearted, if misguided, hope of admonishing him into ease. "Come Darcy," he said jovially, "I must have you dance. I hate to see you standing about by yourself in this stupid manner. You had much better dance."

"I certainly shall not," Darcy replied emphatically. "You know how I detest it unless I'm particularly acquainted with my partner. At an assembly such as this, it would be insupportable. Your sisters are engaged and there is not another woman in the room whom it would not be a punishment to me to stand up with." He suppressed a shudder at the notion.

"I would not be so fastidious as you are for a kingdom!" Bingley cried in amusement, both at the irony of his statement, for never was he near as fastidious as Darcy, and at his friend's predictably taciturn behavior. "Upon my honor I never saw so many pleasant girls in my life as I have this evening and there are several of them you see uncommonly pretty."

"You are dancing with the only handsome girl in the room," Darcy declared with a glance in her direction. Inwardly he acknowledged that she was nearly the only woman he could remember noticing at all, so preoccupied was he with his own awkward predicament.

"Oh she is the most beautiful creature I ever beheld! But there is one of her sisters sitting down just behind you, who is very pretty and I dare say very agreeable. Do let me ask my partner to introduce you."

"Which do you mean?" and turning around, Darcy saw a dark haired woman, of shorter stature than her sister, just perceptively tapping her foot in time to the music as she watched the dancers. She did not possess the impressive beauty of her sister, yet his quick mind was struck by the cheerful liveliness of her appearance. This lady did not pine over sitting out the set, sulking like so many women he had observed. No indeed – rather than languishing she displayed an easy pleasure in her surroundings and a generous goodwill towards those enjoying the dance. Darcy wished he could be so content, so able to relish his chosen role of spectator. He knew it to be the safest place for him. Were he to seek an introduction at this juncture it would, undoubt-edly, incite unwelcome attention and gossip while forcing him to indulge in idle conversation with a young lady whose companionship surely must be intolerable. Why should he subject himself to such atrocities? A dance was entirely unthinkable. He moved to turn back round in order to give Bingley a decidedly negative response to his proposal when the lady's eyes locked on his and he realized, with a great deal of horrified mortification, that she had obviously overheard Bingley's idiotic suggestion!

She gave him a knowing look – he could almost read her thoughts: "Well sir? Would you deem my company insupportable?" There was no denying the challenge implied in the raised brow: she was clearly calling him out. Was retreat possible for a man such as he? To not step forward now would be ungentlemanly, an insult to what he must admit to be an intriguing young lady – unthinkable! If there was anything certain to overcome Darcy's timidity it was the need to always uphold the dictates of etiquette. Why else would he have come to this unfortunate assembly in the first place? He was a Darcy of Pemberley after all, descendant of some of the oldest families in England, nephew to the Earl of _____. He had the honor of his name to uphold; it didn't matter if it meant attending an assembly with his host or preventing the infliction of an insult upon a lady, he would fulfill his duty.

"Very well Bingley. If your partner would be so kind, I would be happy to make the acquaintance of her sister."

⁕

Elizabeth Bennet was, to put it rather mildly, surprised when approached by the intriguing and handsome Mr. Darcy. Rumor had it he was amongst the wealthiest gentlemen in the land and was, to all appearances, extremely displeased with his provincial company and unlikely to oblige anyone with his attention. She had indeed overheard his conversation with Mr. Bingley and smilingly seethed at the man's dismissive manners. She prepared herself for what she perceived as the inevitable blow of rejection by lifting her chin, directing her gaze, and embracing a satirical perspective on the reticent gentleman. If nothing else, experience told her that such impertinence would readily drive off even willing partners, not draw them to her side. For a moment their eyes met but she failed to catch Mr. Darcy's response to his friend. Assuming it was not in her favor, she returned her regard to the dance. But here was an uncanny circumstance! For suddenly there he was, presented to her with all due ceremony by her sister Jane, "My dear Elizabeth, may I present Mr. Fitzwilliam Darcy. Mr. Darcy, this is my sister, Miss Elizabeth Bennet."

"Miss Elizabeth," he began smoothly, if quietly, "it is a pleasure."

"The pleasure is mine Mr. Darcy." She curtsied prettily.

"Are you available for the next set? I would be honored if you would grant me your hand."

"Certainly sir. I am indeed available."

Darcy released the breath he had been holding, unobserved of course. The worst was over: the introduction made. He bowed and retreated from further conversation, waiting nervously for the dance to commence and praying it would not prove too tedious a trial to bear.

Elizabeth pulled Jane aside. "Did Mr. Darcy request this introduction or has his fine friend coerced him into it?" she eagerly inquired.

"Of course not Lizzy! Mr. Bingley assures me Mr. Darcy is everything amiable, only it seems he is a bit timid in a crowd."

"Why should such a man as he be ill-qualified to recommend himself to strangers?"

Jane gazed at her sister, imploring her to be kind to Mr. Bingley's friend.

"Very well," Elizabeth responded to the silent request. "He is decidedly handsome. I shall not be such a simpleton as to allow myself to appear unpleasant to a man of such consequence."

The ladies would have enjoyed laughing at this characteristic retort of Elizabeth's had not the next set begun to form and their partners presented themselves. Mr. Darcy braced himself against the curious stares of onlookers as he led Miss Elizabeth to the floor, but he could not ignore the hum of speculation as Meryton stood in wonder at the withdrawn stranger's singling out of the second daughter of Longbourn. He focused on this lady as the dance commenced, hoping to block out both his discomfort and the gossiping company.

In this endeavor Darcy found himself surprisingly successful. In Elizabeth's eyes he recognized a calm acceptance of his attentions, not the flirtatious idiocy with which he was so often confronted on the dance floor. She smiled becomingly in response to his gaze but seemed, having completed the basic preliminaries, not inclined towards conversation. Despite his instincts, Darcy actually forgot himself a bit and relished the rare pleasure of enjoying a dance: be assured – a most unusual occurrence.

Elizabeth noticed her companion's discomfort as they took to the floor and began to feel some pity for him, struggling as he was to conceal his vexation with the poorly concealed murmurs of her neighbors. Certainly this was not a man made smug by his position – rarely had she encountered anyone so ill at ease. Remembering her promise to make herself agreeable, she thought to initiate conversation but could not escape her own thoughts long enough to proceed. As he silently but expertly led her through the dance, she regretted the part she played in unwittingly provoking him into an uncomfortable situation. If only she had been less proud in her response to the overheard conversation – she was, after all, an eavesdropper, though be it an unwilling one, and thus deserved to hear something unflattering to herself. Yet it seemed that instead of being appropriately knocked down by her transgression, she was instead the subject of all her neighbors envy! The least she could do in return for such felicitous entertainment was not to torture the man with idle conversation. And so she never attempted it; they danced in a mutual and agreeable hush.

It did not escape Darcy that, though he could relish a silent dance, his partner might take offense at his total lack of conversation. As the first song ended he gathered himself to the task of making a rather mundane comment on the performance of the dance. Miss Elizabeth responded only vaguely, as befit the statement, finding that even with her rather extensive communication skills she was at a loss for a retort to such insipidly polite conversation. Mr. Darcy winced. He could only imagine how turgid he must appear to this attractive young woman, she who had been kind enough not to overwhelm him with just such humdrum chatter as he had been blubbering. Struggling for a smile, he strove to redeem himself, "It is your turn to say something Miss Elizabeth. I talked of the dance, now you ought to remark on the number of couples."

Completely surprised that the quiet man could suddenly prove witty, Elizabeth smiled back and said with an arch look, "What do you think of books?"

"Delightful," he replied, suddenly feeling more composed, "much better than the usual ballroom conversations. Shall we pursue Richardson? He is a favorite of mine. But perhaps Shakespeare is more appropriate to the occasion?"

Elizabeth, though noting with approval her partner's literary taste, could not resist making a mischievous retort. "As you like, sir," she challenged, "though acknowledging that 'brevity is the soul of wit,' perhaps I should execute mine by continuing to hold my tongue."

Perish the thought! It became him to concede, "If the Bard himself can be harnessed towards such an unfortunate end, Miss Elizabeth, we really must abandon the topic of books altogether." Elizabeth – it was a name he had always favored and enjoyed using it. How fortunate that she was a younger sister! They must not continue in silence now. "Having already covered the dance, what is there left we can discuss but the weather? Perhaps our health?" Darcy almost laughed at his own jest, so much was he enjoying the novelty of playing interrogator as, typically, his statements were intended to block conversation, not encourage it. But he was soon to discover that novelty is very short lived, if not regretted, as the dancer's roles reversed with Elizabeth's mischievous response: "Do you talk by rule then, when dancing?"

"Obviously not!" he emphatically thought. But who could not be astonishingly intrigued by the humorous glint in what he now recognized as a set of extraordinarily fine, dark eyes? Quite unthinkingly and totally unlike himself, he admitted, "As our dance has amply demonstrated, most certainly not!" They both laughingly accepted the evident truth of this statement.

"Did I just make a joke at my own expense?" Darcy wondered in amazement. Even more striking was that he found himself unconcerned by the self-inflicted jab, so comfortable was he with this lady he had only just met. Befuddling really, when so many women he had known for years continued to make him uncomfortable – Bingley's sister Caroline amongst them. He found his partner's next comment, calculated in kindness to sooth any blow to his dignity, terribly gratifying, "Sometimes a silent dance, well executed of course, can prove far more satisfying than one marked by the strain of broken small talk."

"Indeed. Perhaps that is why society was wise enough not to be too stringent in its regulation of this area. Now that we have canvassed the topics allowed us we may happily forgo all further pleasantries, should we so choose." Though they grinned at each other in amusement, neither wished to pursue such a course. They parted in the dance.

Elizabeth was greatly enjoying herself. Not only did she appreciate the blessing of a graceful dance partner but also the gratification of vanity in receiving such flattering attention from the most distinguished quarter she had ever encountered. But her happiness was threatened when, just as she regained her partner, she observed over his shoulder her mother, from the far side of the crowded room, determinedly striding towards the dance floor with their neighbor, Lady Lucas, in tow. The ladies positioned themselves near the dancers and proceeded to whisper furiously to one another – little doubt did Elizabeth have as to the nature of this conversation. For as long as she could remember, her mother had spoken of none but two topics: her nerves and the disposal of daughters. That the eyes of Mr. Darcy, a single man of immensely large fortune, should fall upon herself was certainly propelling both topics to new heights of interest for Mrs. Bennet.

Chapter 2

"Now what do you make of this?" that lady exclaimed triumphantly to an ever-patient Lady Lucas. "I must say I always knew Jane's beauty would attract a wealthy man, if one should be so fortunate as to fall in her path, but I certainly never harbored such hopes for Lizzy! Not that I'm complaining, mind you. If Mr. Darcy should take it into his head to fall in love with my daughter it would be very fortunate indeed. I just hope Lizzy minds what she says. No need scaring him off with that tongue of hers. She can be entirely too much like Mr. Bennet sometimes and I can assure you, my dear, that a particularly becoming young lady he would not make!"

"Calm now, Mrs. Bennet. Miss Eliza has charming manners; a witty word of hers has never trespassed decorum. Surely you have nothing to fear – Mr. Darcy seems quite taken." As these words were spoken, Lady Lucas' eyes were fixed across the room where the two youngest Bennet girls, Catherine (Kitty as all called her) and Lydia, were predictably dancing raucously with their partners. "No," she thought, "Lizzy will not be the Bennet who frightens away potential suitors. Someone, I know not who, should take those girls in hand."

Of course Mrs. Bennet and Lady Lucas were not the only ones whose attention was drawn to the elegant couple at the top of the line.

The seemingly haughty Mr. Darcy's favoring of a much-beloved local lady easily rendered this the most exciting assembly of the season. Even Mrs. Long scaled down her previous assessment of his manners: when she had attempted to speak with him earlier, she believed he deliberately snubbed her, but now she was convinced that the man must be hard of hearing on the right, a sad ailment for one so young, "Miss Elizabeth best think twice of an alliance with such a prematurely deteriorating man, ten thousand a year not withstanding. He seems hale enough now but one never knows what the future might bring. She may well find herself tied for years to the sickbed. I knew of a young lady who found herself in just such a predicament; she thought she was very well married but not a year into the match her husband fell ill. She spent years nursing him, wasting her youth, and when the unfortunate man finally died found herself right back where she began, with nothing but her dowry to live on as everything went to his younger brother!" The entire neighborhood was suddenly highly interested in the expectations of Miss Elizabeth Bennet.

"Kitty!" Lydia called out as they passed each other in the dance "Do look at Lizzy! She is dancing with that handsome Mr. Darcy."

Kitty, to her great chagrin, missed a step as she surveyed the line, but any embarrassment she felt was swept away with elation for her sister. "Oh, my how exciting! Mrs. Long told me he has twice Mr. Bingley's income. I do hope he falls in love with Lizzy!" Silently she wondered if she might ever be so distinguished, her heart slightly aflutter with the notion.

Despite such rampant general interest, perhaps only one person in the room could be deemed as concerned as Mrs. Bennet with this surprising development. For Caroline Bingley, the sight of Mr. Darcy, a man who professed to deplore a ball, dancing with one of the local

girls was disturbing enough to cause her face to flush with consterna-
tion. The effect was not becoming. Upon first perceiving the pair she
hurried to her sister's side, ignored the appearance of her next dance
partner on her right, and proceeded to interrogate her sister, Mrs.
Hurst, regarding the identity of her favorite's partner.

"Louisa, you must know the name of that lady dancing with poor
Mr. Darcy! How ever did she inveigle him into such an unpleasant
predicament?"

Mrs. Hurst surveyed her sister carefully, taking in the jealous glint
in her eyes, before gazing towards the lady in question, "I believe she
is one of the Bennet girls and that Charles made the introduction. As
you can surely see as well as I can Caroline, Mr. Darcy does not appear
to be distressed." In fact she could not say she had ever before seen
him so at ease in public.

"Oh no Louisa, you are most certainly mistaken! He looks distinctly
uncomfortable. And is not Bennet the name of that vulgar woman, the
one thrusting daughters at Charles? In such unrefined company, Mr.
Darcy must be suffering! Look, there she is now, standing by and
ready to pounce on the poor man. Surely we must endeavor to relieve
him from such an encroachment?"

"He is his own man, Caroline. We must trust him to fend for
himself." So disconcerted was Miss Bingley that she failed to notice as
her would-be dance partner inconspicuously backed away, anxious no
longer to dance with the neighborhood's new heiress but to share his
marvel that the fashionable Miss Bingley was so undone by Meryton's
own Lizzy Bennet instead!

To all this Darcy remained oblivious; for perhaps the first time in
his life, he was blissfully ignorant of the scrutiny of others. Even he
was surprised by his transformative reaction to Elizabeth's simple

courtesy: never had a young lady, other than his sister of course, not treated him as some stellar prize to be won. Darcy looked down into his partner's face as they came together at the end of the set and bestowed a smile of sincere gratitude. Elizabeth smiled back, the honest pleasure she betrayed causing his to broaden. He led her to the side of the floor, fortunately choosing that opposite from Mrs. Bennet, where they were met by Elizabeth's next partner. They thanked each other for the pleasure and parted, Mr. Darcy feeling immensely gratified with the evening and even contemplating, fleetingly, the notion of offering his hand to another Hertfordshire maid.

Elizabeth watched him retreat with a sense of relief for, at that timely moment, her mother made her descent, snatching her away from Mr. Lucas (who was, coincidently, the same patient partner who had been engaged to Miss Bingley for the last) before they could take their place on the floor.

"Oh my dear, dear Lizzy! Mr. Darcy is such a charming man! So handsome and tall! Ten thousand a year I'm told, plus probably more! Oh I do hope you endeavored to please him my dear. Just think, if he should marry you, how grand you would be!"

Elizabeth looked wearily at her mother as she erupted with excitement. "It was only a dance, Mama, and not even a very lively one at that. Mr. Darcy seems gentlemanly and agreeable but he certainly displayed no signs of being smitten."

"This is no time to vex me child! It is up to you to make him smitten of course! You must put yourself forward and perhaps he will ask for a second dance."

"You must excuse me, ma'am, but this dance is already promised."

Mr. Darcy had returned to his former station and resumed his survey of the assembly, now casting a visibly more amiable mien on the room. The dance had been most agreeable, far beyond his expectations which, you will easily recall, were decidedly negative and he felt himself more generous in his estimation of the assembly as a whole. Knowing that the neighborhood could boast of some pleasant and sophisticated companionship relieved the entire company of much of its tedium.

Miss Elizabeth had proved to be a most pleasant partner indeed. He watched her as she moved down the dance – though his critical eye was forced to acknowledge more than one failure of perfect symmetry in her form, her figure was light and pleasing. He wished to know more of her and determined to further the acquaintance. As Bingley was blatantly enraptured with the eldest Miss Bennet (he was, at that moment, soliciting her hand for a second dance), Darcy perceived it would be an easy resolution to which to adhere.

"I must thank you for introducing Darcy to your sister," Bingley said to Jane as they took their places on the floor. "Never have I seen him enjoy a dance more."

"I am pleased to have been of service, Mr. Bingley. Lizzy has always excelled at putting people at ease."

"I wish more people shared her talent. Sadly, while Darcy always receives a great deal of notice wherever he goes, he would much rather go unobserved. In small, intimate groups he fares much better and is exceedingly charming, but in large gatherings he always seems to recede into himself."

Jane Bennet smiled happily at the handsome man, charmed by the affection and care he displayed for his friend, the honor of his attention, and the excitement of that bestowed on her favorite sister. Never had she so thoroughly enjoyed an assembly.

Chapter 3

The evening, altogether, had exceedingly pleased the entire Bennet family. Mary, our missing middle Bennet, had heard herself mentioned to Miss Bingley as the most accomplished girl in the neighborhood, both Kitty and Lydia had been fortunate enough to never be without partners – all they had yet learned to care for in a ball, and upon their arrival home at Longbourn Mr. Bennet found that he too, like his happy daughters, could wish the assembly had never ended as he found himself assaulted by his wife's raptures over the triumphant evening.

"Oh Mr. Bennet! Never have I had such a night! Our girls so distinguished! The entire neighborhood bore witness to their success! I always told you our girls were beautiful for a reason – it shall be the making of them, I've often said it. I have no doubt that the gentlemen will come courting soon and will undoubtedly be completely taken with Jane and Lizzy! Mr. Darcy is so exceedingly handsome! Oh, I just knew how it would be! Such an honor!"

"Just a moment there Mrs. Bennet," her husband interrupted her. "Am I to understand that it is my Lizzy who has caused such excitement? Who is this Mr. Darcy and what ever became of Mr. Bingley, the cause of so much recent uproar?"

"Mr. Darcy," his wife replied with much impatience," is the gentleman whom Mr. Bingley brought back with him from London, of course! Along with his two sisters and the elder's husband."

"I see the rumors of six ladies were quite unfounded?"

"Oh Mr. Bennet, please listen!" Mrs. Bennet pleaded, not betraying her gratification at this sorry but, nonetheless, novel display of interest from her husband in her matchmaking schemes. "Mr. Darcy is the most handsome and eligible young man fortune could have placed in our path! All distinction and elegance! He is said to have ten thousand pounds, Mr. Bennet – ten thousand a year do you hear!"

"How could I not?" he managed nonchalantly.

"He has a magnificent estate in Derbyshire and is surely the finest gentleman in that country, wherever it is. I am sure he must be. Noble lineage too! And the only lady he partnered all night, excepting those in his own party, was our Lizzy!" She grinned triumphantly.

Mr. Bennet, not for the first time, noted his wife's occasional resemblance to a cat, right now one who had caught a particularly meaty mouse. He was almost, but not quite, inclined to pet her. "I see how it is Mrs. Bennet – a rich man has danced with Lizzy. When he arrives to ask for her hand do show him in."

"Yes he surely will come, mark my words. You were not there, Mr. Bennet. You did not witness the attention he bestowed on her!"

"And what of Mr. Bingley? Was he not to your liking?"

"Mr. Bingley is everything amiable. He danced twice with Jane. Twice! It was a most delightful evening! I told you how it would be Mr. Bennet – we shall have Jane settled at Netherfield and Lizzy amongst the first in the kingdom! Surely they will find admirable husbands for their sisters, perhaps even amongst the peerage!" She gasped for breath.

Despite the humor Mr. Bennet always found in his wife's antics he remained quite capable of filtering out anything valuable from her constant effusions. While he was never inclined to become overly heated himself, he did recognize the opportunity these new acquaintances provided for his daughters. "If any deserve it, Jane and Lizzy do," he thought with a chuckle. The notion that the troubling lack-of-an-heir dilemma could possibly be resolved so conveniently to himself as his wife prophesied was an excessively diverting notion indeed. Mr. Darcy had yet to prove himself worthy of Lizzy but, as he had already shown the good sense to single her out, Mr. Bennet would happily acknowledge that as a mark in his favor.

❧

When Jane and Elizabeth were alone the former, who had been cautious in her praise of Mr. Bingley before, expressed to her sister how very much she admired him.

"He is just what a young man ought to be," Jane happily exclaimed, "sensible, good humored, lively!" Elizabeth could not help but laugh. Rarely had she seen Jane so nearly approach giddiness. "And what say you of Mr. Darcy?" the elder sister continued. "I believe I have never before seen such a distinguished gentleman."

Elizabeth did not immediately answer, though well she knew that Jane could detect the train of her thoughts. Similarly, when Elizabeth did speak, Jane perfectly perceived the concern hidden behind her sister's teasing response: "Certainly distinguished – I cannot but admit that I found his company pleasant. That is, when he actually spoke. At one point I grew quite concerned that he had suddenly gone mute between requesting my hand and leading me to the floor."

"Oh Lizzy, you jest! Surely he was not so very quiet."

"I assure you neither of us spoke a word throughout the majority of the dance. Please, whatever you do, do not let Mama hear of it! Her nerves surely cannot handle the shock."

"Yet you found his company pleasant," Jane asserted with a happy smile.

Again, Elizabeth had no ready response. Obviously Jane did not intend to be dodged on this point and, while Elizabeth did keep some secrets from her sister, they were very few. Her admiration for Mr. Darcy need not be one of them, "He is one of the handsomest men I have ever encountered." As she leaned forward to confess this her eyes sparkled. The sisters spent the next several moments indulging in a great deal of incoherent giggling and swooning, quite in the manner of Kitty and Lydia, and far too unbefitting the dignity of both ladies to recount here. Their raptures only ceased when Elizabeth resumed a serious tone.

"I know I should not say so, and would never admit this to anyone other than yourself, but I must confess my great relief Mr. Darcy did not appear to observe the over-exuberance of our mother's reaction to his attentions. I cannot but recognize that a man like Mr. Darcy, not only in his refinement but also his quiet nature, will be quite mortified by her response to him when they finally do interact. I make no pretension at having truly won Mr. Darcy's favor, yet cannot help but regret the opinion he must surely form of our family after she accosts him with her expectations."

"Our mother means well, Mr. Darcy will surely recognize that."

"No Jane, he will not. There is not only our mother to consider. What of Kitty and Lydia? Tonight they behaved even more unseemly than usual, dancing and flirting with complete abandon. No. It was a most memorable assembly but I believe I best not allow myself to indulge in fantasy. I cannot imagine a man of Mr. Darcy's stature marrying a dowerless young lady. What would his relations say?!"

This thought caused both ladies to entertain many melancholy reflections. Jane wondered how Mr. Bingley's relatives would regard her as a potential wife. Already he had been perfectly amiable with Mrs. Bennet but his sisters – well, they seemed less friendly. Jane had experienced a brief but uncomfortable conversation with Miss Bingley that evening in which she was intrusively direct in her questions regarding the size and wealth of the Longbourn estate. Though she would never say so aloud, she was not what Jane could wish for in a sister.

Elizabeth saw her sister's disquietude and made another attempt to laugh at the whims of fate rather than be daunted, "No matter what occurs, I shall not be the one to reject any overtures of friendship Mr. Darcy may extend. I believe I can bear our family's foibles with grace and not be too mortified when he proves to be less swept off his feet than our mother believes. But on the other hand," she grinned playfully, "in the off chance it should turn out that he is subject to such an unfortunate bout of clumsiness, perhaps I can adapt to that circumstance as well."

"My dear Lizzy," Jane laughed. Both ladies fell asleep smiling, more content than uneasy.

❧

At Netherfield, too, the evening was recounted with a mix of excitement and apprehension. Bingley declared that he never conceived of an angel more beautiful than Miss Bennet; never had he met with pleasanter people or prettier girls in his life. Darcy, with characteristic reserve, allowed the evening had been pleasant and the company more worthy than he had anticipated. As both men agreed that the Bennet sisters were charming, Miss Bingley found that she could no longer remain silent. She must interject. Miss Bennet she acknowledged to be a sweet girl – which her brother interpreted as leave to like her – but she could not truthfully claim to have seen any beauty in Miss Elizabeth. She began to recount a litany of flaws in far more detail than it seemed possible to compose after such a brief meeting, covering her face, which was deemed too thin, its features (decidedly unhandsome), and her complexion, which was lacking brilliancy.

Darcy listened in astonishment, taken totally aback that this woman, whom he had always at least considered well-mannered, would so blatantly reveal her pettiness and jealousy. He was amply cognizant that she had long ago "set her cap at him", as the vulgar phrase it, and while tolerating her company for Bingley's sake he had been cautious never to allow himself to behave in any way which might be construed as encouraging her hopes. So his conscience was clear as he mentally rebuked Miss Bingley's ridiculous behavior. After all, what had Miss Elizabeth done but dance with him and what of significance could possibly be gleaned from that?

It was Mr. Bingley, and rightly so, who put an end to his sister's diatribe, "Come now Caroline, she is nothing of the sort. Clearly you are out of sorts this evening. You must be exhausted from having attended an assembly right on the heels of a bumpy carriage ride, though a short one. I'm sure we all are. Perhaps we should retire for the evening?"

The company followed their host's advice, Caroline feeling the sting of her brother's open rebuke. She realized she had revealed far too much of her emotions and resolved to guard against such behavior again. Exposing herself to such a degree was not the best means of dealing with Miss Elizabeth Bennet, nor would it endear her to Mr. Darcy's affections. Subtlety was called for. She would proceed with care.

Chapter 4

The ladies of Longbourn soon waited on those of Netherfield. Miss Bingley did her best to maintain an appearance of civility throughout the visit though she found the mother intolerable, the younger sisters ridiculous, and Elizabeth impertinent. Nevertheless, the visit was returned in due form, providing the Bennet ladies with their opportunity to assess Miss Bingley. She was universally deemed proud and haughty.

"I see no reason why she should put on such airs," Lydia exclaimed. "If I were an unmarried woman at her age I believe I should shroud myself in shame."

"As should I," Kitty readily concurred.

"Mrs. Hurst is more than civil," admonished Elizabeth. "If we must speak of the visit let us speak of her."

"We must grant Miss Bingley some leeway girls," Mrs. Bennet said, ignoring her wisest daughter. "Think of how she must feel. If Jane should marry Mr. Bingley she shall be mistress of Netherfield and Miss Bingley will feel the loss of place acutely, I am sure."

"La Mama! Why should we care for her pains?"

"Your attitude is uncharitable Lydia. We must endeavor to care for the sufferings of all mankind," Mary sermonized.

Lydia rolled her eyes and Kitty giggled.

In the carriage, Mrs. Hurst nodded absently in response to her sister's declarations that only Miss Bennet, of the entire family, was to be borne. Privately, Louisa had grown quite tired of Caroline's jealousy. Miss Elizabeth was certainly a bit of an oddity but she was perfectly ladylike. It would not be a great match for Mr. Darcy, should he actually pursue such a course, but what did that matter to her? She was thoroughly sick of Caroline's ever more obvious attempts to engage Mr. Darcy's attention and shamed by the increasing disdain with which they were dismissed. She was almost convinced that it might not be such a bad thing for Caroline to observe his attentiveness to another woman, even though such an occurrence would undoubtedly prolong the suffering of her own poor ears. Perhaps then her sister would finally abandon such a transparently futile pursuit.

So it was that Mrs. Hurst observed the continuation of Mr. Darcy's attentions to Elizabeth Bennet with a degree of pleasure. Darcy himself was unsure of his feelings but took solace in two, he believed, incontestable facts: the first, that he would never do anything to compromise a lady's reputation by giving her false hope and the second, that Mrs. Bennet (whose company, as is inevitable in a small community, he had now been repeatedly forced to endure) provided ample evidence that Miss Elizabeth, however much he admired her, would never be an acceptable wife. In spite of what Mr. Darcy perceived as the irrefutable soundness of his reasoning, to his dismay he learned that his intentions had already been completely misconstrued by several members of the community, most notably by Miss Bingley and Mrs. Bennet herself.

"Oh, Mr. Darcy! It is such a pleasure!" the latter lady exclaimed upon introduction. "I cannot tell you how I have longed to make your acquaintance, ever since you favored my dear little Lizzy with your hand at the assembly! I cannot account for how we managed to miss each other." Darcy noticed Elizabeth look away and slightly redden. Amused, he wondered if she had somehow maneuvered his previous avoidance of this connection. "And may I say, my dear sir, that you are just as handsome and distinguished as Lizzy claimed. How much she has told us of you!"

"Mama!" Elizabeth exclaimed, her complexion a deeper shade of red. Darcy had a hard time believing it himself, but he found he was forced to stifle a great snort of laughter. In the idea of Miss Elizabeth carrying on about a man in such a way, let alone allowing such a loquacious family to be privy to any feelings she might have in that quarter, he found much humor. All with eyes could see that Elizabeth Bennet, like Fitzwilliam Darcy, highly valued her privacy. Admonishing himself for such unaccustomed humor, he focused on feeling sorry for Elizabeth's predicament as her mother rambled on. It wasn't until later, when he retired for the evening, that Darcy realized he had entirely forgotten, so concerned was he for Elizabeth, to feel on his own behalf the embarrassment of being assaulted by the most blatantly matchmaking mother he had ever had the misfortune to encounter. How remarkable (and gratifying) that mother and daughter should be so dramatically different!

Despite her awkward family, every encounter between Elizabeth and Darcy strengthened the latter's opinion of this Hertforshire lady. One might argue that in a limited society, the few people of intelligence will naturally seek each other's company. Together they find a reprieve from the folly of lesser minds. This is, in fact, a line of reasoning both Darcy and Elizabeth frequently employed during this time as a rationalization for their mutual attraction. But while Darcy had the solace of his two incontestable facts to rely on, Elizabeth had only her fear of disappointment in love with which to guard her heart, a stalwart but still pregnable form of defense.

"Not you too!" she was forced to admonish her friend, Charlotte Lucas, upon being questioned about her feelings for Mr. Darcy. "From so many others I expect such fanciful notions, not from my practical Charlotte!"

"There is no use denying it Eliza. What other woman does he notice? Only Mr. Bingley could be more overt in his attentions."

"What a comparison to make! I assure you Mr. Darcy and I are friendly, nothing more, while Mr. Bingley, as you can see, is most decided in his portrayal of a lover."

"Bingley likes your sister, undoubtedly. But he may never do more than like her, if she does not help him on. The same is true for you and Mr. Darcy." It was the evening of Sir William Lucas' party and the eldest daughter of the house was determined to not allow her best friend to waste such an opportunity for advantageous marriage as that packaged in the form of Mr. Darcy. "My mother is full of your mother's tales of the notice he has paid you. If you make sure he knows how agreeable you find his companionship – and come now Eliza, how could you not? – it will assist his inclination towards you to grow."

"Charlotte, I am not in pursuit of Mr. Darcy! Indeed, I am convinced that our current friendliness depends upon that fact. Nothing would put an end to our civilities faster than my displaying romantic attachment. Mr. Darcy has too much honor to toy with a lady's affections."

Charlotte needed no more information – had Elizabeth felt nothing but the friendship she professed for Mr. Darcy, she never would have even considered the consequences of sharing that sentiment with him. The situation was difficult and Charlotte sympathized with Elizabeth's desire to protect herself. After all, a bridge between the second daughter of Longbourn and the master of Pemberley need span lineage, society, and ten thousand pounds! No small feat indeed. But if marriage was not a probable outcome, it was still a possibility. It may cause Elizabeth some heartache but Charlotte would do whatever she could to improve the odds. She began by asking Elizabeth to entertain the company on the pianoforte, knowing her friend played with a charming and unaffected air, if not always with the utmost proficiency. Charlotte was rightfully gratified when her efforts produced a small but sincere smile of admiration on Mr. Darcy's face. If only it hadn't faded so quickly when Mary succeeded to her sister's seat! The middle Bennet sister was far more diligent in her practice than Elizabeth but had failed to achieve the same natural grace at the instrument. Her performance was pedantic: the lengthy concerto causing her audience more strain than pleasure. Mr. Darcy listened politely despite his distaste for the display.

Mary sat not comfortably but leaning forward at an awkward angle, straining to read her music as her hands moved stiffly across the keys. Though she strove to focus all her attention on the complicated piece, she could not but be aware that her audience was not fully attentive. For perhaps the thousandth time she wished she had the easy manner of her elder sister. If only the world would appreciate her mastery of music more than her appearance when playing! She determined to allot an additional half hour to her daily practice and redoubled her efforts to block out the increasingly noisy room, hunching yet further over the key board in the process.

The polite applause at the end of the piece soothed Mary, who chose to interpret it as a demonstration of some members of the party's good taste. Lydia put herself forward with a call for dancing. Mary felt that

Scotch and Irish airs were frivolous but was flattered by the request to retain her station as performer and so obliged. "A lady must always be accommodating," she thought to herself with a slight smile before commencing.

Along with some of the Lucases and two or three of the officers from the _____ Shire Militia, recently quartered in Meryton for the winter, Lydia and Kitty excitedly rushed to form a set. The latter, however, felt her glee somewhat checked when she noticed Mr. Darcy frowning severely in her direction. That gentleman had been lauded by her mother as the most distinguished man in the kingdom and while she remained happy to indulge her high spirits in an impromptu dance with a dashing officer in his red coat, she could not help feeling subdued by Mr. Darcy's display of censure. Lydia, oblivious to most things, continued to carry on as raucously as ever.

Chapter 5

"Surely these girls are not ready for public display," thought Darcy. "They should be in the school room learning proper decorum, not unleashed to wreck havoc on polite society!" The flirtatiousness of one of the young Bennets was particularly unnerving. He could not recall which girl was Kitty and which Lydia but he had the uncomfortable feeling that the one laughing shrilly while tripping into the arms of her partner was the youngest. Younger even than his sister Georgiana! Such were Darcy's reflections when Sir William Lucas decided to share with him his approbation for the dancers.

"What a charming amusement for young people this is, Mr. Darcy! There is nothing like dancing after all. I consider it as one of the first refinements of polished societies."

"But surely, sir, you cannot believe that such spontaneous antics should be instigated by the very youngest of a party?" He hoped someone, anyone, would assert some restraint on their activities. Nothing good could possibly derive from such neglected manners, especially in young women! This he knew all too well.

"I see where you are Mr. Darcy, I do indeed sir, and let me assure you there is no fear of impropriety here! Not amongst such good friends! In London nothing of the kind would suit. Oh no sir, it would not suit at all. But here in the country we may be more casual. Do you often dance at St. James, Mr. Darcy?"

"Almost never." As Sir Lucas would clearly be of no assistance, he'd rather not continue the conversation.

"Well your friend performs delightfully," noting Bingley, with a nod in his direction, taking a place across from Jane Bennet in the impromptu set.

"Just like him," Darcy thought in irritation.

"I am sure you are adept at the science yourself, Mr. Darcy," the older man went on. Darcy only nodded in reply, hoping to put an end to his interminable chatter. But just as he began to plot his escape from Sir Lucas, unexpectedly the man himself offered a very pleasant one. Elizabeth was at that moment walking by and he called out to her, fueled by the gossip to which he, too, was of course privy, to perform what he considered an inspired feat of gallantry, becoming his role as host and title of Knight. "My dear Miss Eliza, why are you not dancing? Mr. Darcy, you must allow me to present this young lady as a very desirable partner."

Sir Lucas smiled knowingly at the two as Elizabeth blushed deeply, causing Darcy to move to alleviate her discomfort, "Perhaps Miss Elizabeth would prefer to join me for some refreshment?" She smiled her consent and they moved off towards the tea things, leaving Sir Lucas content that he had done his share to further the budding romance that was the talk of the neighborhood.

Darcy and Elizabeth surveyed the typical topics of polite conversation as they sat in a quiet corner over their tea. The weather, their health, and that of their relatives was discussed in form. Upon inquiry, Darcy went into some detail regarding his sister's pursuits before they fell into silence, not an uncomfortable one, mind you, but a companionable silence which Elizabeth, increasingly alarmed by the notable attentions they were receiving from her neighbors, chose to interrupt with this odd little pronouncement: "Mr. Darcy, you must allow me to apologize for the behavior of my many well-intended well wishers. While they will misconstrue our interactions, I wish to assure you that I understand the nature of our friendship, appreciate it, and seek no further claim on your affections." Perhaps she was driven by a perverse impulse to thwart Charlotte's earlier suggestions or by a desire to bolster her weakening defenses against possible future disappointment. Either way, Elizabeth smiled at Mr. Darcy sheepishly as she concluded, feeling quite nervous at her own boldness in initiating such a frank topic of conversation.

Darcy managed to return the smile despite his dismay. How shocking that he should feel so hurt by her words when he himself had been desperately searching for a way to address the same awkward subject! Gathering himself he replied, "There is no need for you to apologize for the actions of those you cannot control. I am well aware of the, ah," hesitating for a moment, "excitement should I say? that people often exhibit towards me. Whether I like it or not, I'm always being subjected to some kind of matchmaking scheme or another." He flushed at the acknowledgment, once again surprised by how unconstrained he felt with Elizabeth. Never with any woman other than Georgiana, and once his mother, had he discussed his highly desirable (or, in the latter case, incipient) bachelorhood.

Elizabeth was overcome by regret for her words and the discomfort, which she so easily perceived behind Mr. Darcy's calm mien, that they had caused. She felt an enormous desire to sooth and protect him from the worries of his status. "So much for emergency defenses!" she thought, ridiculing her own foolishness and scolding herself into better behavior. This was Mr. Darcy of Pemberley, after all. She was the rural lady, the vulnerable one, the one in need of comfort. In his words she heard confirmation of her earlier assertions to Charlotte regarding his sentiments – he obviously wanted nothing more from her company than a reprieve from the machinations of others. She must stay firm and not entertain such destructive impulses. Never had she felt her heart to be in greater danger.

Mary finally retired from the pianoforte and the dancers applauded, more for their own efforts than for hers, and Elizabeth and Darcy lost the little bit of privacy they had found amongst a general clamoring for refreshment. Excusing herself, Elizabeth moved to attend to her younger sisters. Darcy watched with great admiration as she attempted to redirect the most exuberant into a more dignified pursuit than her current one – teasing an officer by not handing over the cup of coffee she had just poured for him. Elizabeth looked up for a moment and caught his gaze. He smiled and bowed in deference to her efforts: a lonely struggle against her sister's impropriety. She smiled back with a slight twinkle of the eye before ushering the girl out of the room.

"I can guess the subject of your reverie." Darcy turned to see Miss Bingley, smiling knowingly. It was a familiarity he attempted to discourage. "I should imagine not," was his reply, but she would not be thwarted.

"You are either considering how insupportable it would be to pass many evenings in this manner or the charms of your future mother-in-law."

Darcy's entire face betrayed the anger he felt at this implication. How did the woman summon the gall? "Your conjecture is totally wrong, I assure you. A lady's imagination is very rapid; it jumps to the most ridiculous conclusions!" With that he turned directly around and walked away with fierce strides, furious with Miss Bingley and indignant on both his own and Miss Elizabeth's behalf, especially in light of the conversation they had only just concluded. Quite apparently, in spite of both of their good intentions, any interest he showed in her would be totally misconstrued. After the party he recollected the various comments, both subtle and explicit, that he had heard during the course of the evening implying a romance between them. The knowledge that they were innocent (for he, at least, still believed they were) only added to his indignation. It was imperative he consider the possible consequences to her reputation and regulate his attentions accordingly. Many other women in such a predicament would feel her consequence raised by such insinuations, but Miss Elizabeth would be mortified. "Must be mortified," he corrected himself, for surely she was as aware as he of the gossip. "Indeed it was what prompted her speech this evening, a wish to alleviate any concerns I might have regarding her assumptions in the face of such speculation. It is imperative that I repay her consideration by taking better care to guard her reputation."

Chapter 6

Caroline Bingley felt Mr. Darcy's snub most severely and concluded from it that the situation between him and Elizabeth Bennet was far more serious than she had previously believed. Had the gentleman's sensibilities not been engaged, he would have responded to what was meant to be a teasing statement in kind. The only explanation she could find for his severe reaction was that there was truth in her speculation regarding future in-laws, a most disturbing notion. That Mr. Darcy, whom she had pursued so diligently, could within a week show more interest in a mere country nobody than she had been able to evoke from him in several years was humiliating. Miss Bingley was determined to put an end to what she continued to deem a dalliance, though a troubling one, before it grew into something more. The best and, she concluded, the easiest way to achieve her end was to play to his pride; by fully exposing the unsuitable nature of the Bennett family she would undermine their pretense to gentility. She had already, on the evening of the assembly, questioned Jane Bennet regarding the family's financial status, but that lady had proven most reticent. No matter, they certainly knew each other better now, having exchanged the basic civilities at least a half dozen times. Surely Jane would not avoid Caroline's patronage, if offered, or the direct inquiries such affability would empower her to make.

An opportunity arose for her to act on her plan a few days later when the men of Netherfield were engaged to dine with the officers of the militia. Without consulting her sister first, as she imagined Mrs. Hurst would disapprove of the scheme, she hastily penned a missive to Miss Jane Bennet.

My dear friend the note began. A presumptive commencement, if acceptable due to being so very hackneyed, but Caroline was determined to use an artful combination of condescension and exaggeration to achieve her aim. The letter would be part summons, part plea, and part snub:

If you are not so compassionate as to dine today with Louisa and me, we shall be in danger of hating each other for the rest of our lives, for a whole day's tête-à-tête between two women can never end without a quarrel. Come as soon as you can on the receipt of this. My brother and the gentlemen are to dine with the officers.

Yours ever,

Caroline Bingley

Even mild tempered Jane felt the inconsistency between the letter writer's words and her behavior. Though civility dictated that she must, she felt uncomfortable accepting the invitation.

Not so Mrs. Bennet. As soon as Jane had finished reading it aloud to the family while they ate breakfast, her mother snatched the note away, scanned it happily, and proceeded to use it to rapidly fan herself while declaring, "Oh my dear, dear Jane! What a sign of preferment from Mr. Bingley's sisters, though it is very unlucky the gentlemen are dining out."

"I wonder they did not include Lizzy," Kitty innocently mused.

"Hold your tongue child!" Mrs. Bennett scolded. "Of course Miss Bingley and Mrs. Hurst would want to get to know Jane in particular, as it is she who shall be their sister! In fact, I'm certain Mr. Bingley suggested the arrangement himself. That is why the men dine out – in order to give the ladies privacy."

"Please let us not engage in conjecture," pleaded Elizabeth. She had no desire to listen to her mother's grand speculations over the breakfast table as they had already spoiled her dinner the evening before.

"You must be correct, Mama, as it would explain why Aunt Phillips never spoke of it and she knows of all the officers' engagements. It must be a newly formed plan," Lydia surmised, not hearing her elder sister and caring for little in the letter other than the mention of officers.

"Well my dear Jane," Mr. Bennett mercifully broke in, "it seems Mr. Bingley's sisters have the good sense to seek your company. Please respond with my assurances that they need not fear for my consent when their brother asks for your hand, as your mother already had the two of you married off a week ago."

"Oh Mr. Bennet! One would think you delight in vexing me! Things are progressing exactly as they should. Now, Jane dear, you must go on horseback as it promises to rain and then you must stay all night!"

"That would be a good scheme," said Elizabeth, in a harsher tone than she usually employed, "if you were sure they would not offer to send her home." But Mrs. Bennett chose not to heed her and well we know that she had her way. Jane proceeded to Netherfield on horseback, was thoroughly drenched by the anticipated rain, and yet another one of Mrs. Bennet's schemes played out exactly as planned – the small sacrifice of her daughter's health proving a worthwhile investment. Right in the middle of her dinner with the two sisters, as Caroline mercilessly pried into the Bennet family's connections, Jane began to display the alarming symptoms of a cold. Said cold called Elizabeth from Longbourn to Netherfield and, low and behold, Mrs. Bennett had two daughters in residence at that house for the better part of a week! The history books offer few records of generals who have executed campaigns more masterfully than this one by the mistress of Longbourn.

Mere words cannot describe how taken Mr. Darcy was by Elizabeth's appearance when she presented herself in Netherfield's breakfast parlor glowing, disheveled, and anxious to see her sister. His actions will have to attest to the matter: the momentary breathlessness that constricted his chest as she stood before him. Her complexion was brilliant, her eyes glittered, and her forehead was lightly creased with anxiety. Noticing the dirt and mud, indicating the conditions of her journey, he was simultaneously overcome by concern for her well-being and touched by the care for her sister such exertions displayed. Darcy fully comprehended, for the first time, how much more than admiration he felt for Miss Elizabeth Bennet and what danger he was in of losing his heart.

Jane continued feverish later in the day. Mr. Jones recommended rest and draughts for the patient and Darcy seized the opportunity to suggest that the lady's comfort would be better secured if her sister were to remain in residence to nurse her, a fine idea in his host's mind. Despite his previous qualms – the image of Mrs. Bennet still lurked in his head – he had decided to pursue his interest in Elizabeth Bennet and having her at Netherfield was an excellent means to that end. "I only hope that Miss Elizabeth can be convinced to 'understand the nature of our friendship' as I now do," he thought with a hopeful smile, watching as Bingley hurried to speak to his sister about extending the invitation.

Poor Miss Bingley! What a terrible predicament she found herself in when she had to ask her rival to remain as their guest until the unforeseen time when Miss Bennet was recovered. Her plan had certainly gone awry. Through her own machinations, the woman she sought to estrange from Darcy was now thrown into his intimate circle. But she would not allow anyone to observe her discomposure and strove to perform her duties as hostess to the best of her current ability. Louisa stayed near her, not quite trusting Caroline to maintain her civility towards Elizabeth Bennet once the men were out of earshot.

Chapter 7

Elizabeth joined the party for dinner and her immersion into the society of Netherfield began. She found herself seated next to Mr. Hurst and experienced all the enjoyment his conversation could offer – on this particular evening, a terse debate on the merits of ragout. Miss Bingley and Mrs. Hurst flanked Mr. Darcy and the former did her best to monopolize his conversation. The joint efforts of Mr. Bingley, Mr. Darcy, and Mrs. Hurst kept Elizabeth from being completely excluded, which she appreciated, but nevertheless excused herself to attend to Jane as soon as etiquette allowed.

Mere moments after the door closed behind her, Miss Bingley began to regale her not so very eager audience with all the details she had squirreled out of a weakened Jane the previous evening. "These poor Bennett girls! My heart does ache for their predicament – you know Longbourn is entailed on some distant cousin and once the house goes their gentility will truly become questionable. I cannot but imagine that the two eldest will find suitable marriages, though probably beneath them. Yet when one considers their recent behavior, perhaps I should not hold out much hope for even that," she sighed with feigned concern and looked to her sister for assistance but, finding none, continued unabashed. "It seems the family line has long been on the decline. Mr. Bennet made a decidedly poor marriage. Mrs. Bennet's sister is married to an attorney in Meryton named Phillips while her brother resides near Cheapside."

Bingley had listened to his sister with growing indignation and finally could no longer remain silent, "If they had uncles enough to fill all Cheapside it would not make them one jot less agreeable!"

"The quantity has nothing to do with it Charles. My point is that they do not have good connections and it shows in their behavior. Why Louisa, you said yourself that Miss Eliza looked nearly wild when she arrived this morning. Very nonsensical to have come at all, really. Her hair untidy, her petticoat muddy, walking mile upon mile unescorted, above her ankles in dirt! And Miss Bennet, what of her riding here in a storm? What could she mean by it? I must say the entire family seems to display a most countrified indifference to decorum."

Again Bingley sprang to their defense but his sister paid him little heed. She was busy studying Mr. Darcy's reaction to her disclosures but, to her great chagrin, all the man seemed to do was stare intently at the far wall of the dining room. Internally he was angry at the ill-breeding Miss Bingley displayed in her derision of the Bennets. It was wrong to attribute Elizabeth's appearance that morning to anything other than sisterly affection. He still felt his head reel at the memory of her complexion and eyes, brightened by exercise. As for Jane, he had ample opportunity to observe her complacent nature and rightly attributed her means of transport on the previous day to have been the contrivance of a terribly misguided mother. Nevertheless, he was mindful enough of the content of Miss Bingley's words to recognize the obstacles he would face if he entertained his nascent idea of pursuing Elizabeth Bennet. With these thoughts in mind he responded to his friend, "Agreeable or not Charles, their circumstances must very materially lesson their chance of marrying men of consideration in the world."

Miss Bingley heard this with glee, thoroughly misinterpreting Darcy's statement. "I am inclined to think, Mr. Darcy," she said with a sniveling smile that turned his stomach, "that you would not wish to see your sister make such an exhibition as Eliza Bennet did this morning."

"Certainly not. However, as a brother, I can understand the affection that compelled Miss Elizabeth Bennet. As a sister yourself, surely you can too, Miss Bingley?"

Caroline was flustered but undaunted, "Of course, Mr. Darcy, but is it not the aim of the truly refined lady to be dutiful without sacrificing her composure? Surely her sisterly attentions could have been secured through other means. And what of Miss Bennet getting herself into this predicament in the first place? I own great surprise that her parents allowed her to set forth on horseback when it surely promised rain."

"Enough Caroline! I simply will not hear another word uttered against either of the Bennets," Bingley exclaimed. "This is my home and they are my most welcome guests. Never have I met a more amiable lady than Miss Jane Bennet. I suggest you find something to like in her or you may find yourself in quite an uncomfortable position, as I intend to see much of her in the future!"

Miss Bingley reeled. Never since her childhood had her brother spoken to her in such a way. Indeed, it's doubtful the adult Charles Bingley had ever spoken to any one in such a tone. His unaccustomed passion distracted Mr. Hurst from his wine, leading that man to make a rare contribution, and a significant one at that, to the conversation, "What's all this now Charles? Are you planning to marry the girl?"

Bingley, rather taken aback by this turn in the conversation, responded to his brother-in-law the only way her could: with the utmost sincerity. "Never have I met a woman so truly an angel."

"You cannot mean to marry her!" Miss Bingley shrieked. So focused had she been on Darcy and Elizabeth that this development shook her to the core. She looked in panic towards a now more supportive sister who said in a subdued voice, "Surely not Charles. It is your duty to elevate the Bingley name."

"How would marrying Jane Bennet not fulfill my duty?" Truthfully he had never really pursued the idea to the degree it merited but, now that it was open for discussion, he felt perfectly convinced that not a woman on Earth could suit him more. "She may not be well-dowered but the family has been at Longbourn for generations, far longer than the Bingley name has been considered genteel."

"And a fine woman she is Charles," Mr. Hurst raised his glass to Bingley. Despite all his indolence, this simple gesture was enough to silence his wife's opposition.

"Is this not a bit sudden, Bingley?" Mr. Darcy asked. "Can you be sure of your affections? And what of hers?"

"I am sure of mine," was the reply, said with all the conviction of one who has long pondered a notion.

Caroline looked at the two friends in horror as she realized how frequently Darcy and Elizabeth would be in the same company should her brother be married to Jane. This was where she should have focused her attentions! "Charles," her voice quavered, "you cannot be serious. It is simply impossible that you could even consider attaching yourself to such a family! The mother is barely ladylike and the younger sisters are sure to expose themselves in some horrifying manner. You cannot do this to me. As a brother and guardian, Mr. Darcy, you must impress upon Charles the damage such a connection would do to the chances of an unwed sister making an advantageous marriage!"

He hadn't thought of that. What of Georgiana should he marry Elizabeth? How would it affect her? Carefully he regarded Miss Bingley and stated, "Every member of a family is concerned and must be considered when a marriage takes place but I believe, in most cases, familial affection dictates that the persons forming the union have their happiness consulted first and foremost." Turning towards Bingley he asked, "Has Miss Bennet expressed regard for you?"

"I believe so."

"And you are sure of yourself?"

Bingley further straightened his already stiffened spine, "I certainly am."

"Then I wish you well."

"Thank you Darcy."

"But what of the degradation, Mr. Darcy? You must make Charles see reason! Surely you would never ally yourself with such a family?"

As she realized the implication of her words Miss Bingley flushed, as did Darcy. Would he not? He could not say. His anger expressed its vehemence in his reliance on his social status, a thing he hated to fall back on, as a defense, "Surely my position in society is a great deal different than your brother's. You forget what he just acknowledged, that your social status is rather closer to the Bennets than to mine."

The words were spoken icily and though Miss Bingley fully felt their chill she would not relent, "I speak not of heritage but of behavior! The family will never be acceptable in polite society."

Darcy wondered if that were true. If someone would exert some control over the more unruly members of the household, would they be presentable? "Perhaps if Bingley is successful with Miss Bennet he can persuade the father to assert his authority more," he thought, despite the reality that it still wouldn't bridge the social hurdle between them. How would his relations respond to the Bennets? He groaned inwardly. How would the Bennets respond to his grand relations? The very idea was mortifying.

"If you wish to live with me Caroline, you must cease this line of conduct!" Bingley was clearly furious and Darcy felt grateful to him for relieving his need to respond. "I am perfectly capable of deciding for myself and either you will accept my choice or make your home elsewhere."

Caroline stared at her brother aghast. Standing, without a word she exited and retired for the night. She had managed herself into an untenable position: one that offered no hope of ever becoming Mrs. Darcy. He had made himself perfectly clear on that point. Her one solace was the mistaken belief that she must have ruined Elizabeth's chances just as thoroughly as her own.

Chapter 8

When Elizabeth came back downstairs she found all the company but Miss Bingley engrossed in a rather solemn game of cards. The group was clearly discomposed and Mrs. Hurst's apology for her sister's noticeable absence, explaining she retired with a most severe headache, did little to explain the tension in the room. The look Mr. Darcy gave her upon entry, however, filled with apology, pain, and confusion, spoke volumes. Never had he looked at her so, and, to her dismay, Elizabeth almost lost herself in that gaze, starting from her reverie only when Mr. Bingley began inquiring after Jane and making room for her at the table. Having just proved her head not presently suited to gaming, she declined her host's civilities, reported her sister much the same, and opted for a book.

The quietness of the players should have guaranteed attentiveness to her task but when paired with the palpably oppressed atmosphere it had much the opposite effect. Her thoughts drifted from Mr. Darcy and the surprising warmth she experienced when remembering the look he gave her, to the absent Miss Bingley, and then on to Jane, all in a puzzle of conflicting emotion. Something had obviously occurred between the household residents while she was with her sister and that something certainly involved the missing lady. She knew not what had happened but she had a strong suspicion, based on their hostess' undisguised disdain, that she and Jane were at its core.

Mr. Darcy had no difficulty concentrating on the game though his thoughts wandered as rapidly as Elizabeth's. The scene with Miss Bingley had been mortifying but he was glad to know that Bingley was serious in his attentions and would not trifle with Jane Bennet. That would hurt Elizabeth and he realized he could not tolerate such a thing. There she sat at her book, wisely behaving as if oblivious to the strain in the air. He knew not how he would proceed in regards to her, recognizing that if Bingley's intentions should come to fruition he would inevitably find himself often in her company. Should he have to watch her someday marry another ... such an idea had already become too abhorrent for contemplation. Instead he mused over the much more pleasant image of Georgiana having such a wonderful sister as Elizabeth.

Mrs. Hurst's thoughts were on her sibling's unruly behavior, her husband's on the game alone, and her brother's on the path he had declared himself to be pursuing. It pained him to have exchanged such words with Caroline but he was quite certain of the sincerity of his affections. Never before had a lady so totally captivated his heart; with the greatest anxiety he fervently hoped that his admiration was returned.

Eventually Elizabeth abandoned her futile pursuit and returned to Jane, sadly finding her condition considerably worse. Most of that first night at Netherfield was spent at her sister's bedside. By morning, she was highly fatigued but gratified by a noticeable improvement in her patient. Guiltily, Elizabeth acknowledged to herself some selfishness in her relief, as during the worst part of the night she had resolved to alert Mrs. Bennet, upon the morning, to come and assess Jane's condition herself. This sudden improvement surely negated the need and Elizabeth could conceive of no possible benefit to be derived from unnecessarily exposing those at Netherfield to her mother.

Mr. Darcy also suffered a largely sleepless night and would have been gratified he had been spared Mrs. Bennet's presence the next day had he only known of his escape, but other cares troubled his mind as he tossed and turned under the increasingly uncooperative counterpane. "What will the family say," he wondered, "should I present them Miss Elizabeth Bennet as my betrothed?" Georgiana would certainly welcome a companion but he could only grimace at the image of his Aunt Catherine's face. She would undoubtedly be boisterous in her disapproval; surely it was well past time she accepted that he would never marry her daughter Anne. What of his Uncle? His cousins? After getting to know Elizabeth they could not help but approve of her – but what of her family? The grimace deepened. Miss Bingley might have been pleased if she had known of his torment.

Neither Elizabeth nor Darcy, despite their best resolutions, were able to steel themselves against their susceptibility to one another. In each other's company they could only enjoy themselves, in defiance of Elizabeth's vulnerability and Darcy's pride. Miss Bingley, remarkably subdued, avoided any intercourse she could with her unwanted guest, adding relief from the lady of the house's glares to the incentives Darcy had to seek Elizabeth out. He began to wonder if much of her bravado towards himself was a facade as they had, of late, taken to gazing at each other in what he believed to be a tender way. He sincerely wanted the attraction he was experiencing to be mutual though he had no doubts that, should he ask, she would accept his proposal regardless. All the Bennet girls were surely obligated to marry as well as possible: everyone was, including himself. Therein lay his dilemma.

What constitutes a good marriage? Should wealth and breeding be the utmost concern? Many a marriage that perfectly fulfilled the worldly qualification ended in misery, as Darcy had far too often observed, and a lack of refinement was not an accusation that could be leveled at Miss Elizabeth. He marveled at how she maintained her grace and composure in the face of the incivility of her hostess.

"Mr. Darcy, you really must not continue to frown so," Elizabeth admonished. "If you persist you will force me to do something most unbecoming and childish".

"And what would that be," he asked, instantly intrigued.

She spoke softly and conspiratorially, "When no one else is looking I shall stick my tongue out at you!"

He laughed, "Oh how ever will I survive such an attack." Temporarily all his concerns were forgotten. She had a unique and delightful way of causing him to lose himself.

The passing of another day saw Jane well enough to join the party after dinner: Mr. Bingley fawned over her and his sister glowered while, on the other side of the room, Darcy and Elizabeth happily discussed their favorite poets. Observing Elizabeth's approving glance at her sister and Bingley, Darcy decided the time was right to fulfill a determination he had made, upon the evening of Elizabeth's arrival and the declaration of Bingley's intentions, to inquire into the state of Jane's affections.

"Your sister seems much improved."

"Yes," she responded brightly, though he thought he could detect a tinge of regret. "I believe we shall return to Longbourn soon."

"When Miss Bennet has not yet had the opportunity to enjoy her stay?"

"For someone who has been ill she has had a remarkable time I assure you," Elizabeth laughed.

"She does seem to enjoy Bingley's company."

"I believe she said he is everything a gentleman should be."

"High praise indeed."

"From Jane it certainly is." She grew serious, "Your friend would not toy with a lady's affections, would he sir?"

He responded in kind, "He has been known to fall in and out of love with great rapidity," Elizabeth frowned and he hurried to reassure her, "but he does seem to be experiencing a most sincere attachment to your sister."

"Does he indeed?" Elizabeth asked excitedly, her sparkle returned.

Darcy laughed, thrilled to see her joy, "I cannot betray my friend's confidence. I have already said far too much."

"So you have, sir, as have I. Shall we resume the much safer subject of poetry?"

In consequence of an agreement between the sisters, Elizabeth wrote to Longbourn requesting the carriage, which her mother promptly denied, requiring her to apply to her host for transportation or risk intruding upon the household (and her reluctant hostess) for an unseemly length of time. Mr. Bingley most emphatically insisted that there was no reason for them to leave so soon, they were more than welcome at Netherfield and surely Miss Bennet was not yet strong enough to depart. The man was so determined to keep the Bennet ladies in his home that Elizabeth acquiesced to remaining one more evening, planning to depart following the morning service on Sunday. Longer than that she could not be induced to remain, largely do to the curtness of her hostess' civilities. Bingley was just thankful to procure himself an additional day of Jane's companionship.

With much contrivance between his friend and staff, Mr. Bingley managed to be alone when Miss Bennet entered the breakfast room the final morning of her stay. He jumped to his feet with all the nervousness befitting a deeply in love man on the precipice of a proposal, "Good morning, Miss Bennet. You look so well I find it hard to imagine you have ever suffered a day of sickness in your life."

"Thank you Mr. Bingley. Good morning to you," she beamed and blushed, flattered by his marked attention.

Shuffling nervously, he waited while she made her selections from the side board and then readily seated her in the place next to himself. A few moments passed in awkward silence before Bingley managed to summon the courage to pronounce his mentally rehearsed speech. "My dear Miss Bennet," he began with all composure he could muster, "I cannot say how sorry I am that your time with us has been the result of illness but, nonetheless, I must admit to cherishing this opportunity to get to know you better. It has been only a few weeks since we met, I know, but I cannot help but say, Miss Bennet, that I have never met a lady who matches you in loveliness. I find myself most sincerely attached to you and would be the happiest of men if only you would consent to be my wife."

Jane looked down, her face scarlet, and quietly said, "Yes Mr. Bingley. I am most honored," before looking up and bestowing on him the most radiant smile he had received from her yet. A few minutes later when Elizabeth and Darcy, having taken a conveniently timed walk, cautiously entered the room, so lost were the happy couple in each other that they did not notice their quiet, approving presence for several moments. Finally spotting her sister, Jane rose from her chair and moved forward to embrace her. "Oh Lizzy, tis by far too much! I do not deserve it. Oh! Why is not everybody so happy!" she exclaimed as Elizabeth laughed, assuring her that she was deserving of all her present joy and a lifetime more. Darcy and Bingley shared a hearty handshake before the latter greeted Elizabeth in kind, as was now his brotherly right. It was a celebratory party Miss Bingley and Mrs. Hurst walked in upon soon after, much to the former's chagrin.

Mr. Bingley escorted the ladies to Longbourn following Matins to request a private conference with Mr. Bennet. Parental consent to the match was expressed readily and simply by Mr. Bennet; Mrs. Bennet's approval was a bit more verbose. "Oh my dear, dear Jane! I am so happy I know not what I shall do! I said how it would be all along – you could not be so beautiful for nothing!" Her sisters too were anxious to share in Jane's joy. Mary petitioned for the use of the library at Netherfield while Kitty and Lydia begged very hard for a ball.

Chapter 9

"I hope, my dear," Mr. Bennet interrupted his wife's wedding plans over breakfast, "that you have ordered a good dinner today because I have reason to suspect an addition to our family party."

"Oh dear, yes. I had not considered that. Mr. Bingley will be joining us and perhaps Mr. Darcy as well! Unfortunately there is not a bit of fish to be got today."

"Actually I put Mr. Bingley off for tonight and, while I cannot say what plans Mr. Darcy may have, I can assure you that it is another gentleman entirely that I am expecting – a stranger whom I never saw in the whole course of my life."

The table came alive with speculation; so successfully had Mr. Bennet ignited his families interest that a few minutes actually went by before they resumed the wedding buzz.

"Perhaps it is one of the officers?" Lydia suggested.

"Or yet another handsome bachelor has entered the neighborhood?" Kitty guessed.

"Fancy three unmarried men of good fortune in one month! When two have been enough to undo us? Surely such bounty is excessive," laughed Elizabeth.

Even Mary commented: "An older gentleman, full of the sobriety and wisdom of his age, would not be unwelcome." How anti-climatic was Mr. William Collins' appearance after such a build up? Severely.

Mrs. Bennet was particularly vexed, somewhat understandably, whenever the estate's entail upon this unknown and uncared for distant cousin was mentioned. But by the time of his arrival, her anticipation of an introduction was only surpassed by Mr. Bennet's, who always delighted in the ridiculous and was certain, by the tone of his letter, that Mr. Collins was a prime specimen. When Mrs. Bennet read the missive, she was more taken with the intimation that he would marry one of her many daughters than with the man's idiocy, which she characteristically failed to perceive. This did much to change her response to Mr. Collins and erased most of the precipitous prejudice she harbored towards him, so that upon his arrival, he found himself quite cordially welcomed by the lady of the house instead of being subjected to her spleen, all traces of animosity temporarily forgotten.

Unfortunately, little was better suited to revive Mrs. Bennet's ill will towards Mr. Collins than to witness the heir of Longbourn's praise of the home's interior, with a poorly disguised eye to future ownership, but the knowledge and security of Jane's good fortune buoyed her spirits. With zeal she announced the recent engagement and relished the disappointment that registered in Mr. Collins' approving eye. Mrs. Bennet might have been oblivious to much but she was keenly observant of any interest displayed by an eligible man in her daughters. Certainly she noticed Mr. Collins turning the focus of his appraisal towards Elizabeth and pettishly looked forward to further frustrating his hopes.

Mr. Bennet was not disappointed in his guest. There was much in which to find amusement that evening as Mr. Collins determinedly set to informing the Bennets of every detail regarding his fortunate situation as rector of Hunsford, his magnanimous patroness Lady Catherine de Bourgh, and her magnificent estate, Rosings Park. Upon having heard enough of this to fully assess Mr. Collins' eligibility, Mrs. Bennet made several attempts to turn the conversation back towards Jane's wedding, which remained her most pressing interest despite the unexpected visitor. Back and forth they attempted to speak over each other and control the tide of conversation, creating quite a racket in the process. Though he had rarely been so thoroughly diverted, even Mr. Bennet's love of the ridiculous had its limits; once he felt his hostly duties had been fulfilled he was happy to redirect his guest's attention, requesting he entertain the ladies by reading aloud while eagerly escaping to his library.

A small conflict arose regarding what Mr. Collins should read, an incident which did nothing to enhance that gentleman's opinion of his two youngest cousins. Fordyce's Sermons was finally selected, to Lydia's great chagrin. Not three pages in she rudely interrupted the reading with a bit of supremely trivial gossip, so affronting Mr. Collins that he almost refused to continue. Though many assurances were given of the audience's attentiveness, he was most stubbornly insistent that he would not read on until Mary placated him thusly: "It has often been observed, sir, that those in the most need of instruction are those who will resist it most fiercely. Surely the greatest attribute of the cler-gyman is his persistence in times of trial, great and small, tending to even the most unwieldy members of the flock."

To everyone's great surprise, this pedantic appeal was received graciously. Mary experienced the rare pleasure of having her words heeded and, though Lydia could only be described as stunned by such an occurrence, Kitty could acknowledge feeling a bit impressed by the middle Bennet girl's rare, if odd, display of social acumen. Jane and

Elizabeth were pleased to see Mary experience some triumph and Mrs. Bennet, in an instant, concocted great plans for her previously least-interesting daughter. And as for Mr. Collins, as he droned on for more than an hour, he had ample time to appreciate his cousin Mary's good sense and attentive, if plain, countenance. He even managed to find a moment to bemoan the loss of such a practical lady, for his purpose at Longbourn was transparently none other than to choose amongst his cousins a wife. Knowing this to be his goal he had already, in his very brief time in the house, determined that Elizabeth would be the recipient of his courtly attentions, this decision made immediately upon learning of Jane's engagement and seeming quite sensible, Elizabeth being next in both birth and beauty. The match would be highly suitable, remarkably convenient, and he had every confidence his cousin would deem it likewise.

⚬⚬⚬

After making such a stalwart resolution one might think that Mr. Collins would have been disheartened the next morning when, upon finding himself tête-à-tête with Mrs. Bennet, he received a caution against pursuit of the very Elizabeth he had fixed on, but then one would not be accounting for the flexibility of this astonishing specimen of humanity. For a conversation beginning with his parsonage house and leading naturally to the avowal of his hopes that a mistress for it might be found at Longbourn, elicited this presumptuous comment from his hostess, "I have reason to believe, sir, that Lizzy's affections are already quite attached to a wealthy gentleman of large fortune who has recently come into the neighborhood, though I know of no existing predisposition amongst my younger daughters."

It was a natural progression for Mr. Collins to turn his sight on the next chronologically eligible daughter, despite some understandable disappointment that the ladies of the house were not as ripe for the picking as he had imagined. There was some minor indignation to overcome as he felt his station entitled him to the pick of the litter, but his eager mind quickly perceived how much more appropriate Mary would be as a companion at Rosings than the elder, more showy Bennet girls. Though not a sensible man, no one would dare underestimate how keenly aware Mr. Collins was of his duty to his illustrious patroness and her daughter; readily he grasped at the notion that Miss Mary would be of far more assistance in upholding his claim that Miss De Bourgh was superior to the handsomest of her sex (and other such homages he thought due the ladies) than a sparkling Miss Elizabeth or breathtaking Miss Bennet.

In many more words than need be recounted here, Mr. Collins assured Mrs. Bennet that he would very much enjoy getting better acquainted with her middle daughter. What were her pursuits and accomplishments? Happily Mrs. Bennet recounted Mary's diligence and piety, suddenly valuing these qualities more than she ever had before. What a surprise blessing a household of daughters could prove to be! Mary was perfect for Mr. Collins – it now appeared that she had been raised purposefully for the role of clergyman's wife and Mrs. Bennet happily took the credit for educating one of her daughters thusly. She treasured up the hint from Mr. Collins and trusted she might soon have three daughters advantageously settled. Mr. Collins, formerly loathed and despised from afar, now stood high in her good graces.

Though Mary was not privy to this conversation she would not have found it disagreeable. It was difficult being the middle child amongst such sisters and she had often experienced great anxiety regarding her desirability. Mrs. Bennet's constant preoccupation with the disposal of her daughters only heightened these concerns: each of the many times her mother bemoaned their fate should Mr. Bennet die, Mary would picture her particular lot in that scenario and saw much to bemoan. Surely her prettier, livelier sisters would make matches of some sort or another but what was she to do? Work as a governess? Spend her life caring for an aging and unloving mother? While she had long ago determined that she would not shirk from fulfilling whatever role life demanded from her, she also prayed fervently that it would be one of wife, not caretaker. So when Mr. Collins began to pay her attentions she felt both flattered and receptive, having rarely been the focus of masculine notice. From her perspective Mr. Collins was an excellent match – she honored his profession, his role as her father's heir, and the good sense he showed in wishing for a practical and pious wife above a beautiful one.

After parting from Mr. Collins, Mrs. Bennet rushed into the library in order to share her good news, "Mr. Bennet! Oh Mr. Bennet it is too perfect!"

"What is it my dear?"

"Mr. Collins of course! He is interested in our Mary! She will make the perfect clergyman's wife and break that odious entail. Have I not arranged everything admirably?"

"It is your affair to arrange as you will, Mrs. Bennet," he replied, barely containing the smile that threatened to destroy his nonchalant mask. "If you desire to live out your years in residence with Mr. Collins the match will of course receive my blessing, but I for one will be glad to be dead, buried, and rid of the man."

"Oh, how you do vex me Mr. Bennet!" she exclaimed before bustling back out the door. Mr. Bennet listened to the sound of her shrill voice as it carried down the hall before standing and moving to the window. There he spent many happy moments envisioning his grandchildren, the future heirs of Longbourn, playing merrily on its ancient lawn.

Thus an unusual courtship began, quite devoid of the usual flirtations. Mr. Collins listened to Mary play, not in order to admire her image but for the felicitation of praising both her execution and dedicated practice, "Lady Catherine is quite convinced that proficiency can only be achieved with much daily diligence." Mary listened to Mr. Collins expound on his many duties at Hunsford with sincere interest, "Your very proper and prudent devotion to your benefactress is highly admirable." Jane saw the transformation that happiness brought to her normally solemn sister's demeanor and rejoiced. Elizabeth also approved of the couple, though she could not but laugh at their passionless discourse. Kitty, while happy for her sister, was peevish enough to wonder why Mr. Collins would look to Mary instead of herself, even though she had not the slightest desire for his attentions, and Lydia was totally perplexed that anyone, even a clergyman, could attend to Mary's quotations and moralizations. Mr. Collins' notice was no loss to her.

Chapter 10

Mr. Bingley spent an entire, seemingly endless day anxiously awaiting the moment when he would be reunited with his betrothed. Of little else could he speak, making life at Netherfield rather awkward with Miss Bingley still refusing to utter a word on the matter and Mr. Darcy even more quiet and brooding than usual. The burden of her brother's spirits therefore fell on Louisa Hurst, who found herself anticipating the moment when Charles could finally set off almost as much as he did. On Tuesday, following breakfast, she became so impatient that she encouraged him to leave as soon as possible, despite the dictates of etiquette. So when it became clear that Mr. Darcy intended to accompany his friend on the visit, in spite of the breach of propriety such an early call entailed, Mrs. Hurst took notice. Unlike so many others, she had not taken Darcy's interest in Elizabeth Bennet to be serious – obviously he liked the girl but the notion of him marrying so far beneath him was ridiculous. Or was it? "If Mr. Darcy should actually marry Elizabeth Bennet," she wondered with a glance at her sulky sister, "it would certainly raise the status of Charles' match." This notion did much to improve her feelings towards her future sister and she decided to go out of her way to extend friendship to the two eldest Bennet ladies – after all, she did have to compensate for Caroline's behavior. Silently she prayed that her sister had given up, once and for all, the notion of being a Darcy but, unfortunately, she had no way of knowing for Caroline had ceased to confide in her.

Bingley also wondered at Darcy's attendance on the Bennets, happy though he was for the company. As they rode towards Meryton he speculated on his friend's intentions. Never before had he seen him establish anything resembling a casual relationship with a new acquaintance. It was years before the two of them developed their current easy friendship and he had known the Bennet family for barely a month. His immediate acceptance of Jane had also been telling. Bingley had expected some disapproval, at least on the grounds of the family's social standing. It would be well worth noting how Darcy continued to respond to Elizabeth Bennet.

Upon entering Meryton they spotted the three youngest ladies of the house to which they were bound chatting amiably in the street with an equal number of unknown gentlemen. Bingley eagerly approached, Darcy in tow, and greeted cheerfully, "Miss Bennet, Miss Kitty, and Miss Lydia! Good morning. We were just on our way to Longbourn. Is the rest of the family at home?"

Darcy wearily surveyed the group, feeling irritated that the ladies seemed to be unchaperoned, when his eyes caught those of one of the men. Wickham! What on earth was he doing here in such company? Could he have sought him out? No, Wickham's look of surprise was sincere, however quickly he managed to compose himself and touch his hat. Darcy barely returned the gesture before he took off in the direction of Longbourn. Mr. Bingley made hasty apologies and followed his friend. "How odd is Mr. Darcy!" he heard Lydia exclaim as he hastened to catch up to the man, "I swear I never have heard him utter a single word beyond greeting! If he were not so handsome and rich he would perhaps seem disagreeable."

"Mr. Darcy?" Mr. Collins inquired.

❧

When Bingley caught up to his friend and saw the perturbation in his face, he chose not to ask the many questions he had regarding such irregular behavior. Fortunately for curiosity's sake, Darcy chose to break the silence on his own, "That man back there Bingley, George Wickham, that man who is amiably endearing himself to your future sisters is well known to me. He is a thorough cad and not to be trusted!"

"Good heavens Darcy!" Bingley exclaimed, taken aback by the ferocity of this pronouncement. "What on earth could he have done? Shall we return and escort them home safely?"

"I intend to speak to Mr. Bennet and inform him of the man's character, so as to prevent further intercourse between him and the family. He is no harm to them upon first acquaintances, as he is not a quick operator; it takes time to insinuate himself into ladies' affections."

Bingley hesitated but asked anyway, "Darcy, who is that man to you?"

"He is the son of my father's old steward. We grew up together at Pemberley."

"And what has he done to so provoke you?"

"There is a lady's honor at stake Bingley. Be patient and when we arrive at Longbourn I will elaborate." They finished the journey in silence, each deeply occupied in his own thoughts. Darcy wasn't sure how much he was willing to tell of Wickham's attempted elopement with Georgiana, but he knew that it certainly did not include her name. He could only hope Wickham would be equally discrete.

Why was he, of all people, in Meryton? There was no accounting for it. Surely the small town had little to offer a man of his tastes, other than easy temptations in the form of flirtatious and innocent young ladies. He grimaced at the thought. Certainly he was duty bound to warn the vulnerable, regardless of the consequences. Too rapidly could he conjure the image of a young Bennet falling for Wickham's charms and finding herself compromised. It would probably be the tall, forward one – Lydia was her name. She would certainly be an easy victim for Wickham, too easy for him to pass on. He wouldn't think twice of the degradation to her or her family, and never would he agree to marry such a dowerless girl. Should he hear talk of an attachment between Darcy and Miss Elizabeth ... no, he could not permit it to happen. Not to Bingley and certainly not to Elizabeth. By the time he entered Longbourn Darcy was grimly determined and requested, almost immediately upon entrance, a private audience with Mr. Bennet.

"Oh Lizzy! Do you think he is asking for your hand?" Mrs. Bennet squealed as the library door closed behind the gentlemen.

"I think not, Mama, as he has never approached me on the subject."

Elizabeth had noted the disturbed countenances of the visitors, particularly apparent in the unaccustomed intensity of the look Darcy gave her upon greeting, as did Jane, who barely had the opportunity to greet her eagerly anticipated fiancé before he was whisked away. Mrs. Bennet continued to happily speculate aloud while the sisters returned to their needlework, anxiously wondering just what could be the matter.

Mr. Bennet could only be amused by the severe seriousness of his guests, particularly as his future son-in-law did not wear a frown well. Nothing he could imagine could possibly be as dire as the spectacle the two men presented and eagerly awaited an explanation. Darcy noted the humor in the man's eyes and prayed he would take his words seriously.

"You must excuse our unceremonious behavior in accosting you this way Mr. Bennet," he began, "but we just now, in Meryton, encountered several of your daughters in the company of a man of most thorough corruption, a true cad. We hurried here to warn you to guard your family against his machinations." The words were spoken with simple and vehement sincerity but, nonetheless, they elicited a broad smile from Mr. Bennet, much to Darcy's dismay.

"I suppose you refer to my heir, Mr. Collins?" the older man asked with chuckle. "He is the gentleman escorting my daughters this morning. While I must admit he does not stand high in my opinion, I have a hard time attributing any real mischief to the man. Surely you must be mistaken."

Darcy blinked in momentary confusion, "Indeed not sir. I refer to Mr. George Wickham, a man whom I have had the misfortune to know all of my life. I know not what brings him to Hertfordshire, but I am quite familiar with his character. He has a long and sordid history of the kind to make fathers of unwed daughters shudder. Please take me seriously sir, for there can be no mistake."

Now Mr. Bennet frowned, a far more welcome expression by Darcy's way of thinking, and he nodded seriously at the older man in approval, grateful his words had made their impact. However, Mr. Bennet was not mearly convinced of the seriousness of the situation: more than he was concerned for the rogue in their midsts, he was interested in why the distant and formal Mr. Darcy had taken it upon himself to deliver such dire tidings. He was displaying an exceptional degree of interest in the well-being of the Bennet family. Mr. Bennet chose his words with care, "I appreciate this intelligence Mr. Darcy. The man's name is Wickham you say? Excuse me, but I cannot help but ask how a man so disreputable came to be known by an honorable gentleman such as yourself?"

Darcy inhaled deeply to steady himself before replying, "Mr. Wickham is the son of a very respectable man who had for many years the management of all the Pemberley estates. We being nearly the same age, I had ample opportunity to observe his vicious propensities. Since both our fathers' deaths, it seemed that all connection between us was dissolved until he intruded himself upon my attention about a year ago, when he was thwarted on the verge of elopement, in connivance with the lady's companion, with a girl of only fifteen years of age. The man has no scruples, no honor; please believe me when I assure you that he is not to be trusted."

"Very well, Mr. Darcy. I shall take care he stays well away from my daughters. Furthermore, I will inquire in town as to the reason for his presence in order to ascertain if it cannot somehow be expedited. If not, my daughters and those of other gentlemen in the neighborhood will be warned to stay clear of the man."

Darcy was noticeably relieved, tension easing from him as he became secure his words had been heeded. But Mr. Bennet felt there was much more that needed to be said. "Mr. Bingley, you must be as anxious to visit with Jane as I know she is with you. Why not join her? I would like to speak a while longer with Mr. Darcy," turning towards him, "if you don't mind lingering, sir?" It seemed Darcy had relaxed too soon.

Chapter 11

"Would you care for a glass of sherry, Mr. Darcy? It is a bit early but, forgive me, you look as if it would be welcome."

"It would sir. Thank you." Darcy was far from knowing what to expect from this interview but he felt confident the conversation would be uncomfortable. A bit of fortification was most welcome. He accepted whatever fate was to be his along with his glass and waited for Mr. Bennet to reveal his intentions.

"So Mr. Darcy," he said, settling back into his desk chair with his drink, "I believe you have more to say."

"Do you indeed, sir?" He had expected the man to begin with a question or trivial comment to ease discussion, some hint of his purpose, not an open invitation to free discourse. Mr. Bennet gave him a knowing smile which made Darcy feel uncannily like a child in trouble, unwilling to admit it, and being taken to task by a seemingly omniscient father. "What does the man expect of me?" he wondered.

Mr. Bennet decided to be blunt, "The concern you have shown today, Mr. Darcy, on behalf of my family is extraordinary. If I paid attention to such things, I might be inclined to attribute your behavior to the rumors of an attachment between yourself and my daughter Elizabeth."

He was right – this would be uncomfortable. Darcy knew not what to say, his feelings on the matter still being very much in turmoil. Mr. Bennet watched him struggle for a response and took pity on him, somewhat, by continuing, "Lizzy holds a special place amongst my children in my affections. Only she is a real companion to me – someone I can converse with who has the quickness, wit, and intelligence required for good company. Despite my wife's behavior, I assure you I am in no rush to dispose of her in marriage and will only do so where I can be assured of her happiness. In the meantime, I may not always be able to provide her with all she deserves but I can, as her father, protect her from danger. And not just the kind posed by the likes of Mr. Wickham, Mr. Darcy. You have shown her attentions beyond what you have demonstrated towards any other lady in the neighborhood and it has given rise to wide speculation. While you have been the utmost gentleman on all occasions, I feel I must warn you, sir, that I cannot allow my daughter's sentiments to be trifled with. So it is that I feel duty bound to ask: what exactly are your intentions towards my Lizzy?"

Though the words were spoken rather gently, Darcy felt nearly asphyxiated with shame. To be on the receiving end of such a lecture from a lady's father – particularly Elizabeth Bennet's father – despite all his best intentions was humiliating in the extreme. But his pride, as always, rallied; he would not shirk this confrontation. As disguise of every sort was his abhorrence, he had little choice but to fully confide in Mr. Bennet.

"I understand your concerns, sir, and share them myself. I have the utmost respect and admiration for both your daughter and her reputation. Never would I do anything to harm her, including toying with her affections. Regarding gossip, if there is anything you would like me to do in order to stem it, I will behave accordingly. Regarding our relationship, let me assure you that Miss Elizabeth herself has declared ours a friendship only. She neither seeks nor expects anything more from me."

The hint of regret in Darcy's voice as he spoke these last words was not lost on Mr. Bennet. He refrained from smirking at the thought of his matchmaking wife's approval as he replied, "I know my daughter well and, as I am sure you have noticed, Mr. Darcy, my home is a bit chaotic. There is very little privacy to be had and Lizzy, in her own defense, has learned to closely guard her feelings, sometimes even from herself. She would never intentionally strive to deceive anyone, but if she instigated such a conversation with you as you recount, I have to imagine she did it in instinctive defensiveness. Had she no stronger feelings for you she would not have bothered; when the gossips grew loud, she would have simply avoided you."

Darcy looked into the man's eyes, noticing how very much like Elizabeth's they were, and felt the truth of his words. Indeed, had he not suspected as much himself? "Dear God! Does she truly return my affection?" he wondered, a churning of anxious happiness swirling inside him before being dashed by a sense of hopelessness so complete it threatened to overwhelm him. He stood and began to pace the room with violent strides.

Mr. Bennet observed Mr. Darcy's obvious torment with some degree of elation. Here was a man in love if he had ever seen one! Mr. Darcy was ideal for Lizzy, everything she deserved, but obviously something stood in his way. Mr. Bennet braced himself to hear what the obstacle was that impeded his daughter's path to happiness, fervently hoping it could be easily overcome.

After many silent moments, Darcy finally stopped pacing and turned to his host, "Mr. Bennet, I must say that your words greatly distresse me. As you have correctly perceived your daughter is of great interest to me – in fact, I believe her to be the handsomest woman of my acquaintance! But sir, you must understand the familial obligations by which I am constrained. My choice of wife is not mine alone to make – I must think of how the connection will affect my sister, my future children, and the well-being of my estate. If it was my feelings alone that had to be considered, the situation would be different, but that is not the case. I must do my duty to my name."

Mr. Bennet was far from pleased with this speech; he felt the inherent insult to himself in the words, but recognized with the wisdom of age that it was not intended as such. Still, he hadn't perceived Mr. Darcy to be such a proud man and instinctively angry words intended to knock the pomposity out of the man threatened to erupt before he checked them. His many years had taught Mr. Bennet better means by which to gain his point. "Am I to understand, sir, that you would sacrifice happiness to your family's social ambitions?" Darcy did not respond. "As one who has lived a bit longer than you have, sir, and has had the advantage of experiencing many years of the married state, let me assure you that what one is convinced one wants in marriage is seldom what one learns, once it's too late, one needs. No monetary reward is large enough to compensate for an unhappy marriage, believe me. Surely an astute young man such as yourself has noticed that my wife and I are ill-matched, though I do love her in my own way. Like so many young men, had I been wiser I would have chosen differently."

Darcy studied the older gentleman – he certainly did see the disparity in his marriage and it seemed to be this lack of harmony that fueled all the issues that abounded at Longbourn. "Please excuse me sir, if I take your tone as an invitation to proceed with similar candor erroneously, but what I have noticed is that you seem to avoid your wife, leaving the care of your children to a lady who is, excuse me again sir, more concerned with marrying off her daughters than raising them correctly. Granted, Miss Elizabeth's position is lower than I imagined for my wife, but I am certainly wealthy enough that her lack of fortune is no constraint. My scruples lie not so much in the monetary but in the proprietary. It pains me to say that I have watched the behavior of your younger daughters on more than one occasion with dismay. You must take them in hand sir, before something irrevocable happens. Indeed, it was all too easy to imagine the most dire consequences for their conduct, seeing them as I did today in the company of George Wickham. Such considerations had much to do with my urgency in speaking with you, Mr. Bennet."

"So there lies the issue," Mr. Bennet thought with a frown. Certainly he could not blame the man. In fact, Mr. Darcy was aptly displaying the wisdom he had just accused him of lacking. Mr. Bennet knew his defects as a parent and landlord; unhappy in marriage, having failed to produce an heir, he was much more content to hide away in his books than to supervise lands his offspring would not inherit or attend to children he mostly found intolerable. Now his indolence was hurting Lizzy, the one child for whom he would not fail to exert himself. Besides, the future looked far brighter with the prospect of a match between Mary and Mr. Collins on the horizon – with Jane and Elizabeth attached to such distinguished gentlemen, perhaps his life would prove a credit to his name after all. His good humor returned.

"What shall I do sir?" he finally replied. "I am but one man alone against a herd of females. You too would find it daunting I warrant. It is easy to feel defeated and retreat from the battle but, provide me with a winning strategy, and I will once again enter the fray and endeavor to bring the house to order."

"I know it must be difficult," Darcy quietly replied. He was pleased that Mr. Bennet did not see fit to reproach him for his intrusiveness, attempting instead to amend the matter. "I have but one sister in my guardianship and despite the most careful attention I still find it to be rocky terrain. With such a large family, it would be impossible to manage on your own. Did you never think to employ a governess?"

"We discussed it when the girls were young but Mrs. Bennet was suspicious of the idea. And what lady, in her right mind, would take such a job at this juncture?"

"It is a bit late to be forcing the ladies into the school room – well, what about that? School I mean. There are many fine institutions that would provide exactly the right environment for young ladies in need of a bit more refinement."

"You know, we did consider school for the girls years ago, but with such a brood the expense seemed unjustified. Now with one daughter soon to be settled," he raised an eyebrow, "perhaps enough income will be freed to at least send Kitty and Lydia. The discourse at Longbourn would certainly improve without them. Why, I might even be able to go an entire day without hearing of redcoats!"

Darcy smiled, relieved to have so positively weathered the encounter. But Mr. Bennet was not done with him quite yet. "So, Mr. Darcy," he said jovially, "with the youngest Bennets safely ensconced in a reputable institution, and if a few words to Mrs. Bennet can curb her enthusiasms, what will you have to say to my Lizzy then?"

Darcy, still not knowing how to respond, was silent, leaving Mr. Bennet to answer his own question, "Time will tell, Mr. Darcy. It always does."

Chapter 12

Time passed slowly for Elizabeth as she endeavored to wait with patience for the interminable hour, during which Mr. Darcy and Mr. Bennet were in conference, to end. Shortly after Mr. Bingley returned, he and Jane departed for a walk on the grounds while Mrs. Bennet bustled away to make dinner preparations, determined to tempt their gentlemen callers, upon learning that they were unengaged for the evening, to remain the entire day with the promise of a sumptuously spread table. So when Mr. Darcy entered the sitting room he found Elizabeth both alone and discomfited. His immediate impulse was to relieve her anxiety.

"Excuse me, Miss Elizabeth. I am not intruding?"

"No indeed sir. I confess I have been waiting most impatiently for your reappearance from the depths of my father's library."

He smiled at her and took a seat. She certainly inherited her humor from her father. "You must be quite alarmed by the odd manner of our arrival this morning. Has Bingley said anything to enlighten you?"

"He has not."

"Very well then. I shall tell you all." He paused to steady himself before again recounting his sad tale. "When passing through Meryton this morning we encountered your sisters in the company of a man with whom I am unfortunately quite familiar: a thoroughly unsavory character. I do not know what brings him here or how long he shall stay, but it was imperative I warn your father to keep him well away from your family as he is known to be a – please excuse the word but no other will do – seducer of impressionable ladies."

"Good heavens, Mr. Darcy!" Elizabeth knew he was of the utmost seriousness but the question was too irrepressible not to be asked, "Surely you do not mean my cousin, Mr. Collins?"

"Who is this Mr. Collins?" Darcy asked, thoroughly confused by the Bennet family's propensity to mistake this unknown person for George Wickham.

But there was no need for Elizabeth to enlighten him as, at that moment, the door to the room flew open and the man himself entered, a breathless and sweaty spectacle, presented a groveling bow to Mr. Darcy, and frantically declared: "Mr. Darcy, you must excuse my failure to recognize you before! It was but moments after your departure that I was made aware of your identity. Please except my humblest apologies, sir."

As Mr. Darcy was now clearly befuddled, Elizabeth stepped forward to perform a proper introduction but her cousin, in his eagerness, was too quick for her to intercede, "I am William Collins, sir, the rector at Hunsford and humble benefactor of your esteemed Aunt, Lady Catherine de Bough's, largess."

This only presented Darcy with a new quandary – what on earth was his aunt's parson doing at Longbourn? Mr. Collins continued to oblige him, "You find me here at Longbourn visiting my gracious cousins. Lady Catherine was most insistent that I attend the family."

Before he could continue Elizabeth managed to interject, "Mr. Collins is my father's heir, Mr. Darcy. Your aunt is Lady Catherine de Bourgh?"

"Yes," he replied in a tone of astonishment. "I knew my aunt had recently appointed a new rector, but I certainly had no idea he was a relation of yours." He gathered himself and nodded an acknowledgment, "Mr. Collins." The man was repeatedly reassuring Mr. Darcy as to the fine state of Lady Catherine's health when Mr. Bennet fortunately entered the room and intervened.

"So there you are Collins. I have several more folios I am anxious to give you the pleasure of enjoying. Please do come along as I have been most impatient for your return." Poor Mr. Collins had no choice but to excuse himself excessively and exit after his host, leaving Darcy and Elizabeth alone to contemplate such an uncanny twist of fate.

Once in the hall Mr. Bennet directed his unhappy guest to continue on to the library while he detained Mrs. Bennet, whom they had met on the verge of reentering the sitting room. "Oh Mr. Bennet!" that lady exclaimed, "What did Mr. Darcy have to say?"

"Calm now my dear, no need to rouse your nerves! I shall give you all the details later but, for now, we have only a moment and you must heed what I say." He paused and gave her a serious look, watching for her eyes to grow wide with attentiveness, "Mr. Darcy has expressed an interest in Lizzy. Hear me out Mrs. Bennet!" he admonished as she threatened to squeal. "He has reservations and is not prepared to declare himself at this juncture. It is imperative that you remember that Mr. Darcy is a reserved, dignified man, who is unaccustomed to the high spirits of our family. We must endeavor not to overwhelm him or he will surely flee. This is how the matter now stands – we all must be quiet, sedate, and on our very best behavior when he is amongst us, do you understand?"

Mrs. Bennet nodded. No lengthier speech could have been better calculated to check her usual exuberance. The couple entered the sitting room together, the lady of the house greeting her guest graciously while her husband smiled in approval. Mr. Bennet was just congratulating himself on being able to demonstrate so soon to Mr. Darcy that his words had been heeded when the good impression he sought to make was totally destroyed by Lydia, predictably, who came racing into the room followed immediately by Kitty and a more sedate Mary. Ignoring all decorum and the presence of a guest, the youngest exclaimed, "Mama! Such news! The most handsome gentleman is enlisting in the militia and he is dining at Aunt Phillips' tomorrow! We were invited for cards and supper – we can go can we not? I shall use the time to great benefit getting to know everything I can about Mr. Wickham!"

Elizabeth observed Darcy pale. So this was the man of whom he spoke! Just like Lydia to fulfill her promise by falling instantly for a scoundrel. But to her great surprise, before her mortification was able to sink in, Mr. Bennet uncharacteristically put his foot down.

"No, Lydia, you will not. You will be spending tomorrow evening at home and I shall send word to Phillips immediately informing him that the man ought not be welcomed into his house."

"But Papa!"

"No conversation is required. You and Kitty go to the front parlor and wait for me there. I have much to discuss with you and will follow shortly. I should like to use my library but, as Collins is occupying it, the parlor will have to suffice. Perhaps you, Mary, could provide your cousin with some assistance until I return?"

"Yes Papa." Astonished into obedience, all three girls left the room.

"And you Lizzy, perhaps Mr. Darcy would care to see the grounds? It will do Mr. Bingley and Jane no lasting harm to have some chaperonage."

Mrs. Bennet watched her husband in amazement. "Well done Mr. Bennet!" she exclaimed after he finished ushering Mr. Darcy and Elizabeth on their way.

"Thank you Mrs. Bennet. I have to agree. Would you care to join me?" He offered her his arm and escorted her through the house, anxious to unfold his next surprise.

❦

The veritable epidemic of love unfolding at Longbourn that day might lead one to believe the emotion contagious. Mary knocked timidly at the library door before entering. "Miss Mary!" Mr. Collins exclaimed with a broad smile. "What a pleasant surprise. I was expecting your father any moment to guide me through a perusal of his more interesting volumes. He has a wonderful library, quite exceptional when one considers the size of the estate, though certainly it pales in comparison to the exquisite library at Rosings. Have I yet told you of Lady Catherine's library, Miss Mary?"

"No sir, you have not, but I have always observed that attentiveness to the proper maintenance of such a facility reflects upon the owner's strength of character."

"Rightly said, Miss Mary. It is certainly the case at Rosings. Did you know that the room boasts all of eight windows?"

"Eight windows? Indeed I did not." Mary did not voice her suspicion that such an excessive quantity of light could not possibly be beneficial to the preservation of books.

"Lady Catherine says the room was specially designed to maximize the glorious sunshine that bestows its light upon the jewel that is Rosings. You really must see the effect to truly appreciate it. A studious lady such as yourself would relish such an experience, I am sure."

"I do love a fine library. One with such comfortable appointments would be a pleasure to use."

A shy silence fell upon the usually ready tongue of Mr. Collins while Mary shifted nervously into a chair. She spoke first, "My father had to attend to a family matter, Mr. Collins. He thought I might be of assistance until he can attend you personally."

"Yes indeed, the folios. There seem to be several fine volumes he has set aside. I would appreciate your attention." The two happily immersed themselves in the books and for several minutes found comfort in each other's company but, as more and more time slipped by, both began to grow uneasy.

"What keeps my father?" Mary silently wondered, becoming deeply concerned about the propriety of remaining alone with Mr. Collins for much longer. How often had she read of the fragility of feminine virtue and how its loss is irretrievable – that only one false step can lead to endless ruin, that a lady's reputation is no less brittle than beautiful, and that she cannot be too much guarded in her behavior towards the undeserving of the other sex? But was Mr. Collins undeserving? She was here at her father's behest, with his cousin and heir, a respectable man of the cloth in favorable position. She decided she would stay put until her father arrived. He would not appreciate her looking for him. Besides, like so many of those sad ladies led astray, she was enjoying herself in spite of the potential consequences.

Mr. Collins thoughts were similarly occupied, though his were focused less on matters of propriety and more on the awkward sensations Mary's close presence produced in him as they bent over their book. He had certainly been attracted to his fair share of ladies but never to the degree that he need forsake the opinion that one comely face was as good as another. It was this very belief that made him so confident a suitable wife could easily be found amongst one of his many unwed cousins. But as he watched Mary's profile, occasionally sensing the brush of her arm against his coat as she turned the pages, he felt something quite different than he had ever experienced before. We need not ponder whether the novelty of his sensations was due to the miraculous power of Cupid's arrow or merely to no lady having ever before encouraged his advances – either way, the end result is the same.

Mr. Collins provided commentary on the volume while Mary listened carefully, though she had read it many times before, occasionally asking astute questions which flattered Mr. Collins. Never before had someone attended to him with such deferential interest, except perhaps in the pulpit. "How did I ever believe her plain?" he wondered, as her eyes sparkled with interest. Instantly the image of the two together at Hunsford, cozy together in his library, which would have to be expanded immediately, made him so crave peaceful domesticity that, without much thought for his words (and he had always intended to put an excessive amount of thought into these words), he dropped the subject of a particularly interesting finch to pose this disjointed question: "Did you know, Miss Mary, that the very Saturday night before I left Hunsford I spent the evening at Rosings, for I am often asked, I should mention, and I do not reckon the notice and kindness of Lady Catherine de Bourgh as among the least of the advantages of my appointment, that very noble lady condescended the very night before my departure – between our pools at quadrille, while Mrs. Jenkinson was arranging Miss De Bough's footstool – to tell me (unasked too!) that I must marry forthwith, that a clergyman like me must marry?"

"No I did not, sir," Mary replied, looking down and blushing furiously.

"She did indeed. My views were directed on Longbourn with this intention, for Lady Catherine had already condescended previously to make known her opinion on this matter, as I am to inherit the estate after the death of your honored father, who I sincerely hope will live many years longer. I could not satisfy myself without resolving to choose a wife from amongst his daughters, that the loss to them might be as little as possible, when the melancholy event takes place." Mr. Collins paused self-consciously, wondering if he was proceeding in a manner all wrong.

"That is very kind of you sir." Mary said quietly, hoping he would continue.

"I do not mean to dwell upon such matters. I have not prepared ahead, as is my wont, my words before proceeding just now. The truth is I am struggling to find the most animated language with which to assure you of the violence of my affection for you, Miss Mary. Almost as soon as I entered the house I singled you out as the companion of my future life. Will you, Mary, marry me?"

It hadn't gone at all the way he would have liked; never had Mr. Collins felt more discomfited in his life, though he often had reason to. He prayed she would simply say yes – he had heard some elegant young ladies might reject the addresses of the man whom they secretly meant to accept and he hoped Mary was not of their kind. He didn't want an elegant young lady who would toy with his affections when they had never before been so vulnerable. He wanted what Lady Catherine wanted: a gentlewoman, active, useful, a Mary Bennet.

"Yes, Mr. Collins," she said simply, "I would be honored."

They smiled at each other with giddy grins before Mr. Collins clasped one of Mary's hands and kissed it. When Mr. Bennet entered the room he found two changed beings: Mary aglow with delight and

Mr. Collins bashful. "It will be a good match," he thought contentedly before laughing aloud and good naturedly clasping Collins on the shoulder.

Chapter 13

Upon exiting the house, Darcy and Elizabeth could see Jane and Bingley wandering aimlessly near the shrubbery. Despite Mr. Bennet's request for chaperonage, without a word they agreed to not disrupt the lovers and discretely headed in the opposite direction. Darcy felt all the awkwardness of Mr. Bennet's maneuvers to get the two alone and, while he was grateful to be so conveniently relieved of the company of most of the Longbourn household, he wasn't sure that he hadn't unleashed a matchmaking monster of far greater proportions than Mrs. Bennet. He was equally unsure what, or how much, the man expected him to relay to Elizabeth, but that lady relieved him of the burden of introducing conversation in her ever charming, sympathetic way, "You must excuse me Mr. Darcy, but I fear I am totally distracted. I know not whether to apologize for my cousin's effusiveness, remark on his uncanny connection to your relation, marvel at my father's behavior, or resume our interrupted discourse on a certain scoundrel you encountered this morning!"

Darcy, though ashamed of his cowardice, took the easy way out, "It is astonishing to learn that my aunt's rector is heir to Longbourn. A remarkable coincidence."

"I must say it begs one to question just what sort of character your esteemed aunt may be – we enjoy Mr. Collins' company through an accident of kinship; I cannot imagine we would have the pleasure were the relationship voluntary." Elizabeth, of course, did not know it was in the process of becoming so.

Mr. Darcy smiled, feeling the easiest he had in hours, "My aunt is quite the character, perhaps even equal to your cousin, from what I have seen of him. They must get on famously. Aunt Catherine surely enjoys her domination over such a fawning minion."

"Our colorful relations aside, Mr. Darcy, I still find my curiosity unsatiated regarding your conference with my father. Indeed it has been inflamed by his subsequently uncharacteristic behavior. I feel as if a plot has been hatched to which I am not privy. Like a spoiled child, I must know all. Will you enlighten me sir?"

Darcy spotted a nearby bench and directed Elizabeth towards it, buying himself a few moments to compose his thoughts. Should he indicate his affections, so recently acknowledged, or just inform her of the details of Wickham's character? How much of Wickham was he willing to tell her? More than he told her father? He looked at Elizabeth as she calmly waited for him to commence. He knew he could trust this woman and could think of no better way to display his affection than by confiding to her his most tightly held secret.

"Thank you for your patience Miss Bennet," he began with a steadying breath. "This is difficult for me. George Wickham is a man I have the misfortune to be intimately acquainted with, as he was the son of my father's steward, a man who was everything he is not. We were raised together, side by side. My father was excessively attentive to George: in gratitude to his father, providing him with a gentleman's education. When we encountered him amongst your sisters this morning, I knew it was imperative that I prevent him from insinuating himself into your society. He is dangerous, playing the role of a gentleman, but do not be fooled for there is nothing gentlemanly about him."

He paused but Elizabeth did not speak. Intuitively, she knew that this was only the beginning of his tale; he was clearly composing himself before the revelation of something dreadful. She braced herself for whatever was to come, ignoring the flutter of happiness she experienced when he looked at her so sincerely. He was reaching out to her for support and she refused to fail him.

"I spoke with your father about a particular incident to illustrate Wickham's untrustworthiness. Last summer I was called upon to prevent his elopement with a fifteen-year-old girl who, God help me, I confess for your ears alone was my very own sister, Georgiana Darcy."

Elizabeth gasped. Darcy watched a medley of emotions play across her face. Astonishment, outrage, and tenderness all betrayed one decisive fact: she cared deeply for both him and his sister. He knew then that he unequivocally loved her, as sure of the fact as he was trusting of her discretion with this sordid tale. He told her of how he unexpectedly arrived in Ramsgate before the planned elopement and Georgiana had confessed all – of how her companion, Mrs. Young, plotted with Wickham to make the impressionable girl believe herself in love and hide it from her brother. It felt as if he were purging himself of their corruption as he shared this burden with Elizabeth. Unthinkingly, he took her hand.

She squeezed back. It was a reflexive gesture of compassion, born simply from an instinct to comfort. They looked into each other's eyes as she began to speak, rather rapidly, "How is your sister now? Is she recovered from such an ordeal? What an utter knave! To play upon his benefactor's daughter, of all people, in such a horrific way, and at such an age!"

Darcy smiled at her indignation; it brought warmth to his soul. Suddenly they became conscious of their clasped hands and dropped them promptly. Both regretted the release the moment after it happened: aware of the lost warmth, an uncomfortable silence ensued. Darcy determinedly gathered himself and replied, "Georgiana was quite shaken, as you can imagine. The incident has increased her natural shyness in public and, in many ways, she is far from recovered. Fortunately, the entire affair remains unknown. I cannot express how thankful I am that I arrived when I did and prevented the worse. I was horribly mistaken in the character of Georgiana's companion. It was a long time, I assure you, before I found someone I considered a suitable replacement. Georgiana has come far under Mrs. Annesley's guidance. Her fate is not in Wickham's hands – I saved her from that wretchedness, at least."

"What is to be done regarding Wickham?"

"Your sister has unfolded his purpose – to join the militia. I know not where he procured the money to buy a commission but am pleased to be assured he did not follow me here. Truthfully, I probably would rather not know from whence the money springs. Your father will no doubt urge Colonel Forster to keep a tight watch on him and the families in the neighborhood will be warned to keep him beyond arms length from their daughters."

"Yes my father, that begs another question," Elizabeth replied. "I hold him in very high esteem, as you know, but he has always been known to be a bit, shall we say, lax in his parenting. This sudden burst of paternal enforcement on his part is quite astounding. Whatever did you say to provoke it?"

Darcy allowed a bashful but playful smile which made Elizabeth's heart race, "Yet you know not the half of it. I imagine that at this moment he is informing your youngest sisters of his intention to send them to school."

Elizabeth truly was all amazement. "What a remarkable man this is," she marveled internally, "who in one hour can so amend my father's ways!" Imagine school – what a wonderful opportunity! "Longbourn will be quiet indeed," she speculated aloud. But she was suspicious of Mr. Darcy's self-satisfied look, "You seem quite proud of this unexpected turn of events, sir."

He responded seriously, "Indeed I am. I admitted to your father my grave concerns that for men like Wickham, your family provides an enticing temptation." It was an honest response, as all Darcy's responses were, but he worried she might take offense at the intimation. She did not, instead noting the implication of such attentive concern on his part, as well as that of the confidential conversation they were having. There was a stubbornness about her that could never bear to be frightened without her courage rising, often in the form of impertinence, to the occasion. She had to know the nature of his feelings for her. "My family certainly is one in which havoc wrecks easily but why do you, Mr. Darcy, take such an active interest in us?"

Her chin was tilted at a defiant angle but her heart pounded so violently she feared he must hear it. Hopes she had been terrified to acknowledge churned mercilessly inside her, creating a roaring cacophony, yet all he noticed was the glorious pride she emanated.

"Miss Elizabeth, please excuse me, but though I have struggled in vain my feelings will not be repressed. You must allow me to tell you how ardently I admire you."

The words were concise, as his tended to be, and could not be misconstrued, but the look that accompanied them could. There she saw both hope and indecision which she rapidly misinterpreted, smothering the fluttering of her aspirations. He saw the shadow pass across her face with concern as she revealed her deepest fears, "But you cannot act on your feelings because of my unfortunate relations." Her chin fell; she could hold it up no longer. "I cannot blame you, sir. My mother, my younger sisters, and, sadly, even my father sometimes – they all demonstrate an inexcusable disregard for propriety. A man of your station should not be subjected to such behavior."

Mr. Darcy almost had the inexcusable urge to laugh, so gleeful did the affection she was unwittingly betraying make him feel. But he constrained himself and instead took her hand, this time with great deliberation. She looked at him in surprise.

"Do you truly think me such a prejudiced man that I cannot bear to be subjected to a bit of folly? In truth, I could wish your family more refined, but then perhaps you would not be who you are. I assure you my affection is sincere and my intentions honorable. I would like permission to call on you that we may have the opportunity to further our friendship, as I now have ardent hope it will prove to be far more than that."

She smiled again, the spark he adored restored to its rightful place in her eyes, "I would like that, Mr. Darcy."

⤜∘⤝

Mrs. Bennet received her wish and the gentlemen remained for dinner, a raucous affair by any estimation. Jane and Bingley glowed as they announced their intention to wed just after Christmas, while Mrs. Bennet's brother and sister Gardiner would still be at Longbourn for their annual visit. Though Mrs. Bennet managed to subdue her enthusiasm for this bit of news under her husbands' admonishing gaze, even Mr. Darcy's presence at her side could not keep her restrained after the next announcement. For as soon as Mr. Collins felt he had sufficiently gained the company's attention, he let it be known, in an extraordinary number of words, that Mary had accepted his humble proposal of marriage and Mr. Bennet provided his blessing. Tears welled in Mrs. Bennet's eyes as she gazed lovingly at her formerly least-regarded daughter, now savior of Longbourn. Mary herself looked positively blooming. Elizabeth felt all the happiness of the moment, having only to wish her mother would be less effusive in her approval. That lady was babbling incoherently to any who would listen about all the wedding details at once, each of Mr. Bennet's meaningful glances totally lost on her. Darcy granted the lady, quite charitably considering that he was now regarding her in the light of a future mother-in-law, surprising leeway on this occasion. Her excitement, he reasoned, was not unwarranted: if her exclamations of happiness were a bit piercing, her feelings were certainly natural and just. Eventually she heeded her husband and calmed down, soon enough to be able to fully relish Mr. Darcy's praise of her table.

Generally, despite its volume, Darcy found the celebratory atmosphere that evening pleasing. Kitty and Lydia engaged in less insipid discourse than usual, largely due to the sudden influx of topics. Mr. Collins was thoroughly distracted with his fiancée and never once accosted him on Lady Catherine's behalf, giving Elizabeth and himself ample opportunity to indulge in the banter that came so easy to them, teasing each other into greater feats of mental gymnastics. The sense of happy domesticity that clung to him as he departed did much to improve his idea of life at Longbourn.

When the Bennets finally retired that eventful day, Mr. Bennet provided his wife with the details of his conversation with Mr. Darcy. He felt exhausted but was thoroughly pleased with himself. So too, obviously, was Mrs. Bennet. Her husband was surprised by how accepting she was of Mr. Darcy's criticisms of herself, softened though they were in his account, but so dazzled was her already overwrought mind by the imagined grandeur of Pemberley that she readily and amiably agreed to mind her manners at all cost. She had a surprising burst of momentary insight – which her husband had to credit her for, having yet to think on the subject himself – when she said, "Can you imagine it Mr. Bennet? With Jane at Netherfield, Mary at Hunsford, and Kitty and Lydia at school, when Mr. Darcy finally proposes to Lizzy it shall be shockingly quiet here!" She babbled on, something about the lord Lydia would surely someday marry, but Mr. Bennet dwelt on her words. Perhaps he had been too hasty in disposing of his daughters but, when one is on such a streak, velocity does make it rather hard to slow down. His consolation was that should Mr. Darcy fail to come to his senses and sweep Elizabeth away she would be a most welcome companion at Longbourn, once abandoned by all but himself and Mrs. Bennet.

Chapter 14

"I cannot wait to attend school!" Kitty gleefully shared her excitement at breakfast the next morning. "Shall we go to London, Papa? It is simply too exciting!"

"London schools are expensive, Kitty. I need to investigate the matter further. Mr. Darcy suggested several institutions with which he is familiar. One in particular sounds promising, located in Cheshire."

"Cheshire!" Lydia shrieked. "Where in the world is that! I'm sure I would much rather remain right here. The militia will remain all winter and besides, even then I am already out, full grown: what have I do to with the schoolroom?"

"I should have been thankful for such an opportunity Lydia. Any young lady so fortunate as to have the option of an education is obligated to take advantage of it," were Mary's words on the subject, said while smiling at Mr. Collins who, in turn, beamed back approvingly before returning with renewed vigor to his plate.

"Leaving the militia is unfortunate," Kitty conceded. "Can we not attend in the fall?"

"No," Mr. Bennet replied firmly, deciding it was kinder to not tease his daughters further, "you shall leave in the New Year. The militia's movements hold no weight in the matter. There is a school in Bath that would be highly suitable. I am familiar with it by reputation and Mr. Darcy has visited it on behalf of a neighbor. He assures me it is well run and appropriate to our station."

Kitty nearly leaped from her seat in joy. "Oh Bath! Really?" she cried. This frequently overlooked member of the Bennet family heartily craved variety, a commodity which Hertfordshire was short on. Naturally high spirited, she attached herself to Lydia at an early age, she being the most diverting, for better or worse, of all the sisters. The prospect of Bath was almost too breathtaking for her to tolerate.

"Surely station matters none to me," Lydia grumbled. "Once Mr. Darcy marries Lizzy no one shall dare look down on us."

"Lydia!" Elizabeth cried in embarrassment as Mr. Collins choked on his drink. He coughed violently into his napkin in an attempt to recover himself while Mary attended him with concern.

"There shall be no more speculation on that point. Mr. Darcy is a gentleman, has proven himself a good friend to our family, and apparently finds Elizabeth's company particularly agreeable. No more shall be said on the matter. We owe Mr. Darcy more than to engage in gossip about him."

"Thank you Papa," Elizabeth said. Mr. Collins, still red in the face, studied her carefully.

"Yes, Lydia dear," an unusually quiet Mrs. Bennet contributed in an exaggeratedly sweet tone, "we must be very respectful of Mr. Darcy sensibilities. Please do your utmost to behave perfectly when he visits today. We do not want to scare him off, do we now?" She smiled at her husband, seeking his approval, but he could not bear to bestow it.

"The nephew of my patroness, Lady Catherine de Bourgh, is expected again today?" Mr. Collins anxiously questioned, his curiosity now thoroughly piqued.

"Oh yes. We expect to see him quite often," Mrs. Bennet said complacently, bestowing an indulgent smile on her second daughter.

"Lydia," Mr. Bennet said directly to her, ignoring his guest's agitation, "school is a great opportunity for you, a privilege only you and Kitty amongst my children are going to receive. An education will provide you with the refinement to intermingle with the best of society. It is not within my power to give you much in way of a portion," he said frankly, "but this will certainly raise your marital prospects."

"I am looking forward to going to school Papa."

"Yes, you have made yourself quite clear on that point, Kitty. Returning to you now, Lydia, I have a feeling you will find as ample distraction in Bath as you do in the militia. In fact, I shudder to think what kind of mischief you could get up to away from home. Surely this must be a pleasant prospect for you?"

"And my dear," added Mrs. Bennet, "think of the new school clothes we shall need to purchase for you."

"Why did I not think of that tactic?" her husband silently wondered.

Lydia brightened a bit, "I suppose I shall somehow bear it. Might I have some new bonnets as well?"

"Whatever assures your amiability on the matter," Mr. Bennet replied, before his wife could assent for him.

It was then that Charlotte Lucas was announced. She had not expected the Bennets to still be breakfasting and hoped to intercept Elizabeth in her morning walk so they could speak privately. There was a casualness in her relationship with the family that enabled her to join the table without awkwardness and wait for her friend to be ready to join her. After only a few minutes, during which she was inundated on all sides with the great news the household currently sported, the ladies were able to abandon noisy Longbourn for the peace and quiet of its grounds.

Charlotte was brimming with questions. She ~~already~~ had already heard rumors of much of the events that had transpired at Longbourn, thanks to the steady stream of missives Mrs. Bennet penned to her sister, Mrs. Phillips, that lady's frequent meetings with Mrs. Long, and the speed of the neighborhood's servants' tongues. "So all the tales that are circulating have some merit," she teased amiably. "Truly it is too much good fortune in one family for the gossips to bear!"

"I think you underestimate their tolerance. They know that in light of our luck, whatever mishap next comes our way will be all the more delightful."

"But I also hear that a third match, of still greater triumph than the others, will very soon spiral the Bennet name to dizzying new heights."

Elizabeth blushed and stopped walking. Charlotte looked at her in amazement. Never before had she seen her friend tongue-tied. "So it is true Eliza!" she gasped.

"No, it is not true, at least not yet," Elizabeth fretted. "Oh! Honestly I know not what will happen. He has indicated his admiration, Charlotte, but not yet spoken of marriage. We have agreed to get to know each other better but already I know that he is the best of men. Whatever shall I do should he not propose?" She laughed nervously.

"Elizabeth," Charlotte looked at her deeply in the face, "you are certain Mr. Darcy would never toy with your affections?"

"Oh no!" Her friend moved away defensively. "He is everything a gentleman ought to be. He has been totally candid with me in all our interactions. It just seems he does not yet know if circumstances will allow him to marry me."

Charlotte required no further elaboration. Like all thinking people of her era, she was inherently aware of the many social barriers that stood between Darcy and Elizabeth. "Does this newly discovered relationship between his aunt and your future brother do anything to ease his path?"

"I do not know. Having never met Lady Catherine, how am I to gage her response to the scenario? From what I have heard, she sounds like an excessively proud woman."

"I have a hard time believing, if Mr. Darcy is the thorough gentleman you claim ..."

"He is Charlotte," Elizabeth assured her.

"... that you will not be engaged shortly. For surely he would not be so bold as to declare his sentiments without every intention of acting upon them. An aunt, no matter how grand, is not an insurmountable obstacle to a man in love."

Elizabeth laughed with affected lightheartedness, "I believe you must be correct." With all her heart she hoped she was.

While the two ladies roamed the shrubbery, Mr. Bingley and Mr. Darcy arrived, once again earlier than precisely polite. Their eagerness was not begrudged, as amply indicated by Mrs. Bennets' obvious delight and the nervously genuflecting Mr. Collins. This eager gentleman quickly greeted the new arrivals, launching into a tedious but coherent request that Mr. Darcy grant him a word in private. His appeal was accepted coldly, a precautionary measure as Darcy feared the man might embark on new effusions if encouraged by any affability.

Having managed to piece together who exactly Miss Elizabeth was believed to be attached to over breakfast, Mr. Collins found himself deeply conflicted. He consulted Mary and it was she who convinced him to request a conference with Mr. Darcy before sending a hasty and potentially unwelcome supplication to Lady Catherine, as had been his initial inclination.

The men were shown into Mr. Bennet's library, that gentleman being busy on the grounds. "Mr. Darcy, let me begin by thanking you for the uncommon condescension you have shown in providing me with these moments of what, I am sure, is your invaluable time." Mr. Darcy clenched his teeth. "The gesture reflects the thorough gentility of your character, as one would expect in a person of such illustrious lineage and as I have often had the privileged of observing in my honored patroness, your aunt, Lady Catherine de Bourgh."

"How can I assist you Mr. Collins?" Darcy cut in, hoping to hurry the man along. He was impatient to visit with Elizabeth, having brought a collection of new poetry to share, only just arrived from London, which he was certain she would enjoy.

Mr. Collins teetered from one foot to the other, apparently trying to find his tongue. Finally he croaked out the following, surprisingly straightforward declaration: "It has come to my attention sir, that there is an uncommon degree of intimacy perceived between yourself and my cousin, Miss Elizabeth Bennet."

"And?" Mr. Darcy demanded, indignantly wondering what gave the man the presumption to question his affairs.

Mr. Collins regained his fluency, "Please do not misunderstand me sir! It is not my intention to incur your displeasure, not a man of your status, but I am in such wretched conflict about what to do under the current circumstances! Furthermore, I have the utmost confidence that a gentleman of your caliber need offer only the briefest of explanations and my conscience will be thoroughly put at ease!"

Silently, for he was in high dudgeon, Darcy indicated that Mr. Collins should continue.

"Having had the honor of being received frequently at Rosings, I have often heard Lady Catherine comment on your engagement to her daughter, Miss Anne de Bourgh," Mr. Collins now spoke in an unusually quiet and subdued tone, fearful of how Mr. Darcy would respond. Ironically, that same fear allowed him to quickly recover something of his usual manner and continue before Mr. Darcy could say a word, "Please believe me sir that I have no wish to pry into your personal affairs, though I have often observed that it is the unique province of the clergyman, alone in society, to do just that. I am torn between loyalty to my patroness and my family, but have every confidence that you will provide a perfectly satisfactory account for what must be a mere misunderstanding, probably on my part, and will assure me most promptly that my concern has been misapplied."

Darcy knew not what to think. Rather than anger with the obviously terrified man before him, he felt mostly pity, well deserved too, for his predicament. How dare Lady Catherine speak of an engagement publicly! It was well past time, regardless of any current matrimonial considerations he may have, that Darcy put an end to his aunt's belief in those that would certainly never materialize. He would start by setting straight her rector, "I assure you, Mr. Collins, that my aunt misspoke regarding this matter. Neither my cousin Anne nor I desire such a match." His words brought home that his complacency in this matter, having always avoided a verbal confrontation with his aunt and allowed her to continue in her false hopes, was not unlike the indolent policy Mr. Bennet pursued in the management of his family. A new wave of empathy for the man overcame Mr. Darcy. Like Mr. Bennet, he would strive to rectify his mistakes. This lazy approach had been nothing more than a disservice to all involved, most particularly his aunt.

As Darcy struggled with his emotions, Mr. Collins was tackling a bevy of his own conflicting conceptions, most prominently, "How could Lady Catherine, the great lady who displayed such unquestionable good sense in her promotion of me, be mistaken?" But Mr. Collins' complex mind was able to willingly accept this astonishing possibility when he reflected that if Darcy were not engaged to Miss Anne de Bourgh, although why anyone would reject such a lady he could not fathom, it would be extraordinarily fortuitous if he married instead the sister of Mr. Collins' very own, soon-to-be wife! Yet that idea too intimidated him, for who was to inform Lady Catherine of her mistake? Certainly not he! To be the bearer of such news! The mere idea turned his skin a sickly pallor.

"Are you alright Mr. Collins?" Darcy inquired, upon he noticing the man's strange hue.

"Yes Mr. Darcy. Thank you sir; your consideration is most amiable. I am just concerned," he coughed, "regarding what you have said, sir, that Lady Catherine will be most displeased by this account. I would not wish to cast doubt on the indubitable veracity of your word, sir, but I would be eternally sorry should your aunt be provoked unnecessarily. Please excuse me if, in my honest pursuit of clarity, I seem excessive, but you are quite certain that you have no intention of fulfilling your engagement to Miss De Bourgh?"

"There is no engagement, Mr. Collins, but I will write to my aunt if that is your concern. In fact I shall do so forthwith. It is my responsibility to rectify the situation; I recognize my role in its creation."

"Oh no, Mr. Darcy, I am sure nothing you have ever done has caused the slightest discomfort to anyone," Mr. Collins assured him, beginning to recover his color. "Your graciousness knows no bounds. I assured my dear Mary that you would have a reasonable explanation for the matter and that there was nothing to fear. Now you have proven me correct. How can I thank you enough Mr. Darcy? I shall so enjoy telling my noble patroness how excellent is her nephew, not that she would ever harbor a doubt otherwise. She has always spoken of you in the most excessively affectionate terms."

"You are welcome, Mr. Collins. If you will now excuse me." Darcy hurried from the room in search of Elizabeth, anxious to escape the uncomfortable interview. Mr. Collins retreated to the music room to interrupt his betrothed's vaunted practice with his good news. Mary would have liked to attend her music presently and thought briefly of reminding Mr. Collins what he had quoted to her regarding Lady Catherine's belief in the importance of diligence. Instead she closed the pianoforte and entered graciously into Mr. Collins' concerns, just as every tract she had ever read on the subject indicated a good wife should.

❦

While Mr. Darcy was suffering through his encounter with Mr. Collins, Mr. Bingley was happily ensconced at Jane Bennet's side, listening to her mother babble on about wedding plans. She checked herself when Mr. Darcy entered the room, greeted him warmly but respectably, and calmly informed him that Elizabeth had not yet returned from her walk with Charlotte Lucas. Not wanting to intrude on a private conversation, he opted to wait with the Bennet family and Bingley rather than aimlessly seeking for the ladies on the grounds. It seemed an innocent decision when made but soon proved regrettable.

When he entered the room it was upon an apparent scene of peaceful domesticity, much like that he had enjoyed the evening before, but without Elizabeth's presence to shield him the imbecility of the conversation was maddening. Never had he heard such extensive conversation about lace! Darcy marveled, for perhaps the thousandth time, at Bingley's amiable forbearance of such nonsense. When Mr. Collins and Mary joined the gathering, the level of noise in the room grew to an unbearable crescendo. Lydia loudly demanded that Kitty give her a particular ribbon despite the fact that Mr. Collins was carrying on in his usual droning manner, as if constantly preaching a sermon. Mary smiled on him approvingly, which only encouraged the man, as he dwelt on the unfortunate brevity of his stay.

"Believe me I feel it most acutely that I have only three days remaining to me in such felicitous company as I have discovered amongst my fair cousins, but the rector of a parish has much to occupy his time. Lady Catherine," he paused to bow in Darcy's direction, "is kind enough to allow me to visit with my relations, but now that I have such happy news to share, it seems clear that a week is all that I can reasonably be spared at this time. I must see to the tithes, in such a manner that both benefits me and offends not my benefactress, I must write my own sermons, and the time that remains is not too much for parish duties, the care and improvement of the parsonage. On the later score, I truly could not be excused if I did not make it as comfortable as possibly." He turned directly towards Mary before continuing, "Lady Catherine has gone so far as to suggest many improvements. I trust you will find your future home perfectly amenable." Again redirecting his discourse towards the entire room, so no one might be so unfortunate as to lose a detail, he proceeded to itemize all the improvements made, focusing at length on the practicality of closet shelves, but Darcy managed to block out most of this. In fact, since Mr. Collins had mentioned his time line for departure, he had heard nothing more. "Three days!" he groaned inwardly, wondering how he could continue to endure the man that long, when it occurred to him that his message to his aunt would best be delivered in person. Indeed, it ought to be dispatched immediately. If he left tomorrow, he could speak with Lady Catherine and be gone again before Mr. Collins returned to Hunsford. The time away from Longbourn would also provide an opportunity for much needed reflection.

This latter thought was lost as Elizabeth and Charlotte entered the room. "Mr. Darcy! What a pleasure it is to see you sir. I hope you have not been waiting long?" The ladies came directly to his side.

"The pleasure is mine, Miss Elizabeth. Have no fear, for we arrived only a short while ago." The warm smile cast in Darcy's direction drove all thoughts of Rosings and those concerned with it from his mind, though he did manage a courteous, "Miss Lucas, good morning," before losing himself completely in the joy of Elizabeth's presence.

"Good morning Mr. Darcy," Charlotte replied, happily noting the connection between himself and her friend before turning her regard to the rest of the room. "Good morning Mr. Bingley. I only came in to ask if Kitty would care to accompany me back to the Lodge and call on my sister Maria. She has been wanting your advise on the gown she plans to trim afresh."

"Oh my! I entirely forgot with all that has transpired. May I Mama?"

"Yes go child. We shall do very well without you. Lydia my dear, do come sit by me and tell us your opinion of these gowns. I think this style will suit Jane very well." Were it not the very latest fashion plates she was called upon to survey, Lydia would quite possibly not have been so compliant.

"I shall just be a moment." Kitty curtsied before hastily departing. Elizabeth greeted Mr. Bingley before she and Charlotte seated themselves near Mr. Darcy, on the far side of the room from Mr. Collins. In spite of the resumed oration, they managed a quiet conversation.

"I'm afraid such a pastime as this must have been most uninteresting to you, Mr. Darcy. Surely, you are up to date on all the latest fashions by now?" Elizabeth playfully got right to the heart of his feelings.

"Indeed. I will be sure to share my vast expertise with my sister on her next trip to the modiste."

"And she will undoubtedly appreciate your expert advice," Charlotte dared to intrude on their flirtatious merriment. "As a sister, I can assure you that there is nothing less welcome than my brother's opinion on ladies dresses." They all laughed.

Kitty reappeared and Miss Lucas took her leave. Mrs. Bennet and Lydia were entirely engrossed in their activity, Mr. Bingley and Jane in each other. As Mr. Collins had finally taken it into his head to follow his future brother's lead and focus his attentions on his intended, Elizabeth and Darcy were afforded some degree of privacy. Darcy summarized his conference with Mr. Collins and his plan to go to Rosings. Despite himself, he felt a bit pleased at her disappointment in his departure. In turn she recognized the compliment implied by his urgency to disabuse Lady Catherine of her faulty notions and could not prevent a flush of pleasure in the knowledge. She understood his present desire not to mention her to his aunt, trusting he knew how to correctly handle his relative. He had feared she would object to this measure and delighted in the confidence she displayed in him. If this wasn't love, both were greatly deceived.

Chapter 15

At Netherfield a distracted Caroline Bingley paced the floors, feeling most put out by a second consecutive day of Darcy absenting himself in favor of the company at Longbourn. Occasionally she would stop to strum on the keys of the pianoforte discordantly, eventually causing her sister to flee from the room. Following one of these impromptu musical interludes, having shut the instrument with a snap of disgust, the butler interrupted her with the announcement that there was a visitor for Mr. Darcy. Upon learning he was not at home, the gentleman had insisted on waiting. The butler handed Miss Bingley a newly printed, elegant card, baring a name she did not recognize. The distraction was welcome and she ordered the man shown in. Pasting a more pleasant look upon her face, she picked up her neglected work and awaited the gentleman's arrival.

Immaculate in his new uniform – boots shining, buttons gleaming – the newly made Lieutenant Wickham was a pleasing vision to Caroline's refined eye, as she was to his. At the moment of his entry, even Miss Bingley could find some merit in Kitty and Lydia Bennet's intense admiration for a red coat. He bowed in a most gentlemanly manner and introduced himself, excusing his intrusion while emphasizing the urgency of his need to see Mr. Darcy. Miss Bingley invited him to sit down before replying, "I am afraid my brother and our guest may not return for several hours. Perhaps I may convey a message on your behalf?"

She watched the handsome face fall before he stood and walked to the window, staring out of it in the same brooding manner she had so often observed in Darcy. "Who is this militia man?" she wondered. "Why would such a gentleman not seek a commission in the regulars? And what is his relationship to Mr. Darcy?"

He moved from the window and returned to his prior seat, bestowing a sad smile on his hostess, "I am afraid, Miss Bingley, that the delicacies of my business with Mr. Darcy cannot be easily expressed in a mere message. But surely, as you presently reside in the same home, you must know Mr. Darcy rather intimately – dare I impose upon you with my troubles?"

"Yes indeed sir. Dare away!" she thought, always eager to learn more about Mr. Darcy, through whatever means. Her audible response, however, was more subtle, "I am always happy to oblige my friends, Mr. Wickham. You pose no imposition."

"Thank you, Miss Bingley. You are graciousness itself." He paused before continuing, taking a moment to gage the effect of his words. "I gather by my admittance here today that you know something of the particular manner of my intimacy with the Darcy family?" he said with an appearance of perfect honesty, though he knew it was most unlikely that Darcy would ever speak of him. He was also armed with a great deal of information regarding the inhabitants of Netherfield, which he had been scrupulously garnering since he encountered Darcy in Meryton.

"I am sorry, sir, but I have never heard your name before this very hour."

"Surely I never thought you would ask me in had you not previously heard my name! Mr. Darcy never speaks of me?"

"At least not to me, sir." The indignation in her tone was not lost on Wickham, who rose again and began to pace the room as if deep in thought. Caroline's mind raced to conclusions as she impatiently waited for him to proceed. An intimate relationship with the Darcy's! Whatever could it be?

When he felt he had adequately built up her suspense, he turned to her with his most endearingly pathetic look, "Please excuse my unforgivable distraction, but I am most saddened. I should depart at once, having already taken up too much of your time. My sorry story would only cause you to lose whatever good opinion of me you may have already formed."

It was too much for her to bear. "Please Mr. Wickham! Obviously you have something of great import on your mind. Again I offer you my services in communicating with Mr. Darcy. We have known each other for many years, for he is a great friend to my brother. I assure you I will be totally discreet." His face momentarily brightened before falling again, noting with satisfaction Miss Bingley's corresponding expressions.

"Forgive me, Miss Bingley," he said tenderly. "In your kindness you have offered your ear to my tale of woe and it is simply too tempting to tell all. You cannot know how badly I want to oblige you, but how can I? And yet, my avenues of hope are so small, I have so few options, how can I refuse?" He paused ponderously. "Very well then. Perhaps you are the very person to offer advice on how to proceed."

"I will do my best," she readily assured him.

He smiled at her enthusiasm. "You see my father was the steward to all the Pemberley estates, underneath the late Mr. Darcy, the best man I ever knew." Caroline's face, despite her ardent effort, betrayed her dismay.

"You wonder how a man educated as myself can be the son of a servant?" She bowed her head and blushed in reply. "I was raised at Pemberley, side by side with Fitz – I mean, Mr. Darcy. His father was a generous man and provided for me amply. As my godfather," Godfather! "he oversaw my education, preparing me for a future in the church. Have you ever been to Pemberley Miss Bingley?"

"Yes, indeed I have. It is a magnificent estate," she replied collectedly, though Wickham could perceive the tinge of longing.

"Then perhaps you are familiar with the small village of Kympton nearby?"

"Yes I am. I believed we dined with the rector during our visit. A Mr. Westover, if I recall."

Again turmoil swept over Wickham's malleable face. He paced once or twice more before saying, with great feeling, "That is the very living that the elder Mr. Darcy intended for me!"

Caroline was shocked, "How can this be? Surely Mr. Darcy would not disregard his father's will?"

"There was an informality in the terms of the bequest and Darcy chose to doubt it – to treat it as a conditional recommendation. Certain it is, that the living became vacant two years ago and that it was given to another man, presumably the one you dined with."

"Dear me how dreadful! I should not think it of Mr. Darcy." Suspiciously, "What could have caused such a massive falling out between two childhood companions?"

"I am afraid, Miss Bingley, that it is a very delicate matter. What indeed could cause the best friend of my youth to cast me off so decidedly, without explanation, without remorse? I have a theory as to what lies at the bottom of this misunderstanding, but I am afraid it involves a lady's honor, so I dare not mention it lightly. This is why I so wished to speak to Darcy. You will reassure me, kind Miss Bingley, of your absolute secrecy?"

"It is undoubted, Mr. Wickham. Please continue."

He managed an on command blush, "It seems that Mr. Darcy was most displeased when Miss Darcy – with whom I have always had a very affectionate, brotherly relationship – in the first throes of her womanhood fancied herself enamored with me." By now he was visibly red, nearly the same shade as his coat: the perfect addition to his performance. Perhaps it's not giving him too much credit to believe the effect was aided by an honest tinge of shame for the intense perversion of this revisionist history, as the best actors do rely on real emotions to perfect their art.

For Caroline Bingley, the many questions this new acquaintance provoked suddenly seemed to have one astonishingly obvious answer. Rapidly her mind jumped to its conclusion: George Wickham was transparently the illegitimate son of the late Mr. Darcy! It made too much sense not to be true! She reasoned thusly: first, there had never been a hint of a scandal about the family and everyone must have a skeleton in the closet somewhere; second, why else would Darcy go to such lengths to separate Georgiana from a long time intimate on the threat of a school girl crush; third, she believed she perceived an uncanny familial resemblance between the men. Mr. Wickham was certainly proving a highly interesting diversion.

Their conversation was interrupted when Mrs. Hurst entered the room, having just been informed that there was a visitor. Introductions were made and the intruder found herself pleasantly surprised by her sister's amiability and cordiality, as her sulkiness had been incessant over the past several days. Upon sharing a communicative look, of the sort Louisa missed, Caroline invited Mr. Wickham to join the sisters for tea. They shared a pleasant afternoon, inviting their new acquaintance to stay for dinner. Even Mr. Hurst was jolly, having found the new Lieutenant to be a formidable partner in cards.

When Darcy and Bingley returned that evening, they were understandably both flabbergasted and dismayed to learn who had been benefiting from Netherfield's hospitality in their absence. Darcy had announced to Bingley his intention to travel to Rosings during their ride home and came upon the party in the drawing room while still discussing his travel arrangements. It was Mrs. Hurst who innocently "let the cat out of the bag", so to speak, by exclaiming that Mr. Darcy would surely not wish to depart now that his old companion had just come amongst them, the estranged nature of that relationship being something to which she was not privy. Mr. Darcy's countenance darkened as he inquired precisely to whom she was referring. Upon having his suspicions confirmed he stormed from the room, leaving Bingley to explain his odd behavior to its remaining, rather astonished, inhabitants.

"Louisa," he began, "am I to understand that Mr. Wickham has been here for the majority of the day, quite comfortably insinuating himself into your good graces?" But it was his other sister who responded to the question, "Yes Charles, that is the correct name of the unfortunate man with whom we became acquainted this afternoon. He has sadly lost the esteem of his former companion and I must say I am shocked to see how readily Mr. Darcy rejects his late father's favorite!"

"Caroline, I know not what Mr. Wickham has said to convince you that such is the case, but I warn you now that I have it directly from Darcy that the man is not to be trusted! I must ask you to cease all contact with him."

"Charles!"

"I am sorry Caroline, but I will be firm in this. He is not welcome in my house; Darcy will not tolerate his presence and nor shall I. He is a known fortune hunter and you should be wary of any attention he has paid you."

"Mighty shame, that," Mr. Hurst piped in. "Rarely have I had such a whist partner. Wickham and I showed the ladies how the game is played, I assure you."

"Be that as it may," Charles responded wearily, "we mustn't have anything to do with the man. His society is thoroughly unsuitable."

"I am surprised to hear you speak so Charles, considering the recent choice you have made. Surely you are in no position to pass judgment on what qualifies as suitable society."

"Caroline!" gasped Louisa but her sister was already out the door and closing it behind her. Her anger grew as she climbed the stairs. How dare Mr. Darcy treat such a transparently good natured man so horribly! Who was he to dictate what company she should or should not keep? He was the one determined to dote like a fool on a country nobody! Against his own brother (for that she was convinced was precisely who George Wickham was), to act in such a fashion was truly abominable. Clearly Mr. Darcy was not the gentleman she had always assumed him to be. Miss Bingley did not pause to consider how she would behave towards an illegitimate offspring nor how satisfying it was to be able to look down upon Mr. Darcy's morality. Her mind was entirely occupied by two subjects: the memory of Wickham's handsome amiability and the degree of vexation it would cause Mr. Darcy were she to thwart her brother's will by pursuing the acquaintance.

Chapter 16

Darcy paced his room disconsolately, debating whether or not circumstances required he postpone the trip so recently planed. This direct encroachment of Wickham upon his notice concerned him greatly; the man was undoubtedly up to something. Darcy was torn between his sense of duty towards his aunt and his determination to prevent Wickham from inflicting further harm upon those for whom he cared. Also, having already bid Elizabeth goodbye, he rightly feared, he would never be able to drag himself away should he not leave now. Even more – his plans had the added incentive of a brief sojourn in London, where he would break the journey, allowing time for a consultation with Georgiana. Recent events had incontestably proven marriage a family event; to proceed without consideration of those who it would most affect was negligent, if not cruel. Time away from Elizabeth and Georgiana's opinion would help him determine his future course.

A servant knocked on the door bearing a request from Bingley to join him in the study. Darcy welcomed the opportunity to discuss the matter and proceeded downstairs immediately. His friend had just poured two glasses of cognac and was sipping his contemplatively. "Please join me Darcy," he said, beckoning to the second glass. Darcy lifted it to his host in silent tribute and enjoyed a soothing inhalation of the drink's bouquet before indulging.

"I have told Caroline that this acquaintance in unacceptable. She is very angry but I believe I made my point."

"I apologize for abandoning you back there Bingley, but confound the man! What was he doing here? How dare he present himself so?"

"It seems he has filled my sister's head with tales of unjust treatment at your hands, Darcy. Such gall is astounding. What could possibly be his motivation?"

"Perhaps just to provoke me, but we should not underestimate how far Wickham will go to achieve that end. I think I should postpone this journey to Rosings until we can determine what he is about."

"No Darcy. There is no need for you to so inconvenience yourself. You have told me what the man is and I will protect my family from his machinations. Its high time I was firmer with Caroline. Letting her continue as she is does none of us any service." Bingley was determined and Darcy felt a good deal of pride in his friend. The time was overdue for him to exert his authority as head of his family.

"Very well then. I will leave tomorrow after an early breakfast." Darcy drained his glass.

So as intended Mr. Darcy departed from Hertfordshire the next morning, comfortably ensconced in Bingley's plush coach, and arrived in London in time to join his sister for tea. The journey provided ample opportunity to hope he had made the right choice in leaving, confidant that he could have changed Bingley's mind about insisting he do so, but he had not wanted to undermine his friend when he was so properly exerting himself. Since their arrival in Hertfordshire, a decided change had overcome Bingley. He was more confident and determined in his actions, presumably a result of Jane Bennet's influence. "This marriage will be excellent for Bingley," he thought smugly and allowed his thoughts to stray from Wickham to the more pleasant topic of Elizabeth for the remainder of his journey.

Georgiana Darcy was both surprised and delighted by her brother's unexpected arrival. Rarely did he travel spontaneously unless there was an emergency to address but she could tell upon first glance, even though Wickham weighed on his mind, that never had her brother been less burdened in his life. There was an unusual swing in his always determined stride that she had not seen before. Closer inspection revealed an excited agitation in his typically somber face. "Something certainly has affected my brother, for the positive," she thought, "but what could possibly have induced such a remarkable change in him?" She counted on being quickly enlightened.

After exchanging the mandatory pleasantries which must be attended to upon any reunion, regardless of their value conversationally, Darcy said, "I stop here on my way to Rosings, where I shall head tomorrow. I would continue tonight but as my aunt has no warning of my arrival, I thought coming upon her in the daylight would be less of a shock. Besides, this arrangement gives me the opportunity to visit with you, my dear. I have much to tell."

"More to tell than why you are off to Rosings? A place you rarely take yourself but for your annual spring visit?" Georgiana asked silently, saying aloud, "It certainly seems you do, Brother."

"I have formed a new acquaintance," he said with such a broad smile that it nearly took his sister aback.

"With whom?"

"A young lady."

"Oh! I see," she replied. Both her brother's behavior and the trip to Rosings began to make sense.

"She is a resident of Hertfordshire, Georgiana. Her father owns a small estate near Netherfield. Bingley is to marry her elder sister in December."

"That is wonderful news," she exclaimed sincerely, her animated smile beaming at Darcy. She had often wondered if her brother had not entertained future hopes for herself and Mr. Bingley and was pleased to see him leave the marriage mart. Though she was fond of Mr. Bingley, she had never felt anything akin to romantic attraction for him, nor did he ever betray any towards her. She suspected Darcy now had much better means of making Bingley his brother and hers as well, a role much better suited to her regard for the man. "I am delighted for him," she said, hoping to soon feel even more delight on behalf of her brother. "What is the bride's name?"

"Jane Bennet, the eldest of five daughters."

"And your young lady?" she asked with a nervous grin.

"Miss Elizabeth Bennet, the second eldest of the house – Longbourn is its name," he enthusiastically replied.

"He does seem smitten!" Georgiana thought as she hung on to every detail of his account.

"We met at a local assembly, the same at which Bingley met Miss Bennet. He harangued me into asking her to dance and quite in spite of myself I found her utterly charming. She is so unlike the women I meet in society, Georgiana; she has none of their air of falsity and connivance. I find her company thoroughly rejuvenating. She is kind, caring, honest, and terribly witty. She makes me feel happier than I have ever been and I have asked to spend more time getting to know her."

"Oh Fitzwilliam! She sounds wonderful. But pray, if your plans are to be courting her, why are you suddenly off to Rosings?"

"You will have great difficulty believing the coincidence. I witnessed it and had a hard time grasping the notion myself. It seems that Aunt Catherine's new rector, a Mr. William Collins, happens to be cousin to the Bennets and heir of their estate. Just this week he became engaged to Mary Bennet, the third sister."

"Love is in abundance at Longbourn," she replied in astonishment.

Darcy laughed, "You know, when I first met the family I was certain that such a frantically matchmaking mother as Mrs. Bennet would frighten away all thinking prospects for her daughters. While it is uncertain if the appellation 'thinking' can be applied to Mr. Collins, I must say I either gravely underestimated her, the charms of her daughters, or the powerful force of her husband, as he has proven himself equally determined, in a far more sophisticated fashion, to achieve the same end."

"How strange you should meet Mr. Collins in Hertfordshire!" Georgiana replied, adopting her brother's teasing tone. "Aunt Catherine will be most disappointed not to have the privilege of making the introduction."

"Indeed she will," he chuckled.

"But it just seems too amazing that your Miss Bennet should so soon be sister to both Charles Bingley and the Rector of Hunsford!"

He nodded in agreement, "I have found the entire experience utterly bewildering, I assure you. Part of my motivation for stopping here, Georgiana, was to have the benefit of your conversation in clearing my mind. My feelings for Miss Elizabeth are unlike any I have previously experienced and I need to be sure of their nature before acting upon them. This is why, when Mr. Collins questioned my intentions towards his cousin, having been told by Aunt Catherine that I am engaged to Anne," Georgiana gasped, "I thought it best to use the opportunity to put an end, once and for all, to my aunt's schemes. It also provided a handy excuse to get away for a few days and visit you, me dear, with the added benefit of relieving me of the odious man's presence."

"He really dared to question your honor?"

"He most certainly did. And out of the kindness of my heart I am relieving Mr. Collins of the burden of informing Lady Catherine himself that I have no intention of marrying Anne. You should have seen him squirm at the notion."

"Can he be so terrible, when you are willing to accommodate him so?"

He frowned and rose to stare out the window while responding, "Generally the inhabitants of Longbourn and their associates are not what I have typically considered desirable company, particularly in the case of Mr. Collins. Mr. Bennet, whom, though a bit indolent, I have found to be a thorough gentleman, has done much of late to check the behavior of his wife and youngest daughters, who should really still be in the schoolroom. Unfortunately, the family unwisely brought out the younger daughters at an abominably young age, while the elder remained unmarried. " He sighed before turning to face her, stating bluntly, "Mrs. Bennet has connections to trade which, unfortunately, are displayed in her lack of tact. Her sister is married to a local attorney and her brother resides near his warehouses in Cheapside."

Georgiana could not but be astonished. Clearly the family was well outside their social sphere and never in her life had Georgiana known her brother to trespass its invisible boundaries. All she could assume was that the lady must be extraordinary.

"The Bennets themselves are genteel, I assure you. Even Mrs. Bennet has remarkably improved since we were first introduced. I know not what Mr. Bennet said to her but she has suddenly become far more subdued in her mannerisms, though she still retains a decided air of over exuberance and obliviousness. The two youngest sisters, Catherine and Lydia, I have very high hopes of being redeemed upon their admission to a finishing school in the new year, a measure I am pleased to have persuaded Mr. Bennet to take. Still, it pains me that only Miss Bennet and Miss Elizabeth are truly refined amongst the brood, but that I can assure you they are. You will like Elizabeth Bennet, Georgiana. I know you will. I have only to wish her familial circumstances were less exceptional."

Georgiana was silent a few moments, pondering all the questions her brother's choice raised. How would their relations respond to such a match, so decidedly beneath what was expected? It mattered not, she determined, for she would remain supportively by her brother's side. If anyone deserved to find happiness it was undoubtedly him. "Fitz-william," she finally piped up, rather timidly, "perhaps you would like me to accompany you to Rosings?"

He was startled. Never had he considered bringing his sister along on such a mission, subjecting her to Lady Catherine's inevitable displeasure, but it was a congenial notion. Georgiana's company would serve as a diversion on the journey and perhaps would mitigate Lady Catherine's ire, as she always delighted in her niece's presence. He also recognized that such a spontaneous suggestion on the part of his sister was a great indicator of improved spirits, which had now been depressed for several months, ever since the unfortunate trip to Ramsgate. More than anything, he was deeply touched by Georgiana's gesture of solidarity.

"Perhaps you believe my attendance would further the burden of an impromptu visit on my aunt?" His sister's voice broke his musings.

"Not at all my dear. Forgive my silence and allow me to implore you: never let Aunt Catherine hear you suggest that her household is not prepared for a surprise visit from the King himself, with his full retinue. On the contrary," his good natured smile banished her concern, "I would greatly enjoy your company and appreciate the offer. Only be sure you want to step into the lion's den with me. I expect our aunt will be most displeased."

But Georgiana remained undaunted. Happily the siblings planned their departure. As they would only be gone three days, it was decided that Mrs. Annesley need not accompany them.

"I will collect you immediately following breakfast."

"And you can tell me more about your new acquaintance during the ride," Georgiana teased.

"I fear I can never tire of that topic." The Darcys parted in unusually high spirits.

Chapter 17

Rain pummelled the Darcey traveling coach as it departed London for Rosings, rendering the ride slow and dreary, but Mr. Darcy kept his sister well entertained by honoring her request to share every detail of his interactions with the extraordinary woman he had met in Hertfordshire. Unfortunately, in order for the account to be complete, it necessitated the inclusion of George Wickham, for he might never have declared his regard for Elizabeth Bennet had that man not made such an unwelcome appearance. He hesitated to mention him but recognized that if Georgiana faced the possibility of finding herself in the same neighborhood as Wickham, say for a wedding perhaps, she best be forewarned. Georgiana took the news quietly, after several thoughtful moments eventually musing, "Perhaps then he has finally done some good in the world, if he helped you recognize your feelings."

Darcy was proud and touched by her charitable response, but deemed it best to steer the conversation back towards more pleasant topics, "Does that mean I have your approval of the lady I have described?"

Eagerly forsaking the unwelcome thought of Wickham, Georgiana reviewed the details she had gathered on Elizabeth Bennet. Though they had never met, she felt instantly enamored with this woman who had such an astonishing effect on her brother, rendering him very nearly giddy. It had been many years since he had been so jovial – how could she not approve? Furthermore, she had always dreaded the idea of Darcy marrying one of the many Miss Bingley's who inhabited their world and a Miss Bingley seemed to be precisely what Miss Bennet was not.

"Oh most assuredly Fitzwilliam." She leaned forward and asked quietly, with an air of secrecy, "Did she really walk three miles in mud to attend her sick sister?"

"She most certainly did and, it must be acknowledged, looked positively delightful upon arrival," he smiled at the remembrance. "That does not mean that you should take to any similar notion should I ever fall ill. Sisterly devotion does not justify her behavior – she should not have proceeded thusly though, I cannot deny, I am awfully glad she did."

"Well I think she sounds like a delightful lady, muddy petticoats and all. Of course, anyone upon whom you could bestow your love must be worthy."

"I feared you might disapprove of her social status."

"You happiness is paramount with me, Brother."

"Miss Bingley just recently regaled me with the many horrors to be borne by an unmarried lady whose brother marries into the Bennet family." He frowned and said quietly, "They certainly can be an unnerving clan."

"But you do intend to ask for her hand?" Georgiana ventured.

"I certainly believe I will, though I have no intention of yet broaching the subject with Aunt Catherine. When I depict her for you, her family and circumstances seem insignificant obstacles: the mere backdrop to a comic theatric. It is in their company that I wonder what foolishness this is I am entertaining. But then Miss Elizabeth walks into the room and I have eyes and ears for no one else. What is a man to do?"

"If you have so many doubts Fitzwilliam, than what madness is this that we pursue – rushing off to Rosings to put an end, once and for all, to Aunt Catherine's matrimonial ambitions? And on behalf of her rector, a man your profess to be adverse to, but whom you indulge for no reason whatsoever other than his relationship to a lady of unsuitable background?"

Darcy gave what for him was a sheepish smile, "I do not believe I ever used the word unsuitable."

"Then why do you hesitate? Never have I observed a lady to have near this effect on you. I have longed for a sister such as you describe. If she is really as wonderful as you say, certainly she will not wait forever for you to make up your mind. She has a duty, after all, especially when one considers her familial circumstances, to marry well. She must find it rather insulting that you look so far down upon her relations; do you really believe she will remain available once another man has expressed his interest?" Georgiana had never spoken to her brother so forcibly and was surprised he did not seem to mind, let alone call an immediate end to the conversation, as she had feared.

"Miss Elizabeth seeks not a mercenary marriage," he replied with a slightest tinge of petulant indignation. "She wants what I do, a loving relationship. Were she able to find one in Hertfordshire, I have no doubt she would already be married. And indeed, she feels much the same about her relations as I do. The poor woman has been suffering their company all her life and I assure you, she is often mortified by it."

The vehemence of his defense only served to convince Georgiana that he had better hurry up and marry the lady. She breathed deeply before proceeding, "Then why not rescue her from her predicament?"

Darcy sighed, "Would marriage rescue her? When you stretch an arm towards a drowning man, the odds are you shall soon both be floundering in the water."

"But we live in Derbyshire, they in Hertfordshire!" Georgiana was beginning to feel exasperated. "Surely you would rarely see her family."

"There is truth in that," he mused reflectively. "When did you become such a wise young lady?"

"I have had the benefit of my brother's excellent example to guide me." They shared a loving smile and the conversation ceased, both siblings consumed with their own thoughts for the remainder of the journey.

⁓⁂⁓

Lady Catherine certainly was surprised by the appearance of her nephew and niece but received them, as expected, with the utmost graciousness. She was quite pleased to see the Darcys – as isolated as she and Anne were in their small, familial circle, she thought on her sister's children almost as if they were her own. These were the bonds of intimacy that she looked forward to solidifying with a marriage between the families. In fact, Lady Catherine chose to regard such a casual form of arrival as none other than a sign of her fondest dream's impending fulfillment.

She explained at length that Anne was spending the day abed, listing her many complaints while Georgiana pondered the irony that Lady Catherine could, simultaneously, be so excessively attentive to her daughter's health and oblivious to the fact that such chronic illness virtually eliminated her marriageability. "I know how anxious you both must be to see Anne," Lady Catherine said with an intelligent look at Darcy, which he very nearly squirmed under, "but she has been most unfortunately indisposed as of late. I have high hopes, however, that she will join us for dinner. She shall, of course, improve with the spring, as she does every year. Anne is under the strict care of an illustrious physician, and Mrs. Jenkinson is most attentive to her comfort. She shall surely soon be thriving once again. You both look hale yourselves – you seemed a bit peekish when last I saw you, Georgiana. How long do you intend to stay?"

Darcy accepted the cup of tea which his aunt had just poured for him, "I am afraid we remain for only two nights, Aunt Catherine."

That lady frowned, "And where do you travel from here?"

"I will return Georgiana to London before continuing on to Hertfordshire, from whence I came."

"Nonsense Darcy! Two evenings is no length of time for a proper visit. Stay out the week and I will be able to introduce you to my new rector who returns tomorrow, having also been visiting in Hertfordshire. I simply must have your opinion of him. Besides, you cannot possibly intend to travel on Sunday!"

There was no point in delaying the inevitable. To disassemble now would be unmanly. He had hoped to delay this conversation until he and his sister had the opportunity to rest from their journey, just in case Lady Catherine was so incensed as to expel them from the house, but saw little choice other than to take advantage of this opening, though he did not relish the thought of having to spend the evening in a crowded and noisy inn.

"I have already had the pleasure of making the acquaintance of Mr. Collins, ma'am. You see I have been visiting my friend Charles Bingley, of whom you have heard me speak. He is recently engaged to be married to the eldest daughter of the house Mr. Collins is to inherit."

Lady Catherine was clearly taken aback by this announcement and not at all pleased, "Very well. I am sorry to lose the opportunity of making the introductions. I have instructed Mr. Collins on the importance of marriage for a man in his position and encouraged him to find an appropriate match amongst his many cousins. It seemed most fitting as the estate is entailed upon him. A wife who already knows the ways of the house will make the transition upon inheritance far smoother. I am chagrined to learn that the eldest is spoken for, as she would be the obvious choice to replace her mother, but I suppose her marriage to Mr. Bingley will raise the family's consequence and so is not to be lamented. I understand there is a bevy of ladies at Longbourn. Surely the second will do as well as the first, as long as her sister's good fortune has not made her too proud. If she is a smart girl, she will marry Mr. Collins and put an end to the entail, a sorry thing for women. The De Bourgh family saw no need for such measures, fortunately for Anne."

Again she looked knowingly at Darcy while he cringed at the thought of Mr. Collins making love to Elizabeth. He would get to the point, "It is actually something said to me by Mr. Collins that brings us here today, Aunt Catherine."

"And what was that Darcy?" Lady Catherine demanded in her customary manner, refreshing her nephew's tea most unsuspectingly.

He took a deep breath before proceeding, "Mr. Collins informed me that you have spoken openly with him of your long held belief that I intend to marry Anne. I understand that this is a treasured notion of yours, Aunt, but I must assure you here and now that neither Anne nor I favor the idea. It would be best for all involved if you would relinquish it altogether."

"Surely you jest!" she exclaimed, though it was evident he did not.

Indignantly she rose from her chair and declared with a stiff spine, "A union between yourself and Anne was the fondest wish of both your mothers! Who else so proper, so fit, to follow in my dear departed sister's footsteps at Pemberley than my very own daughter?"

"But I am not fit, Mother," broke in a strained but determined voice. Lady Catherine turned in shock to see that Anne de Bourgh, her always obedient daughter, had at some point entered the room and stood shakily holding the knob of the door.

"Anne! Why are you downstairs? You shall return to your rooms at once!"

"I heard of our visitors and wanted to greet them properly." She began to move towards her cousins, in doing so revealing a nervous Mrs. Jenkinson teetering anxiously behind her mistress.

"But you are unwell Anne," her mother insisted. "You must not exert yourself so. Mrs. Jenkinson, see her back to her room immediately."

"I am afraid, Mother, that as this conversation intimately involves me, I will not be kept out of it." Darcy and Georgiana stepped forward to greet her as warmly as possible, considering the tension all were feeling. Anne took a seat as Lady Catherine continued to stare at her daughter with a bizarre mixture of outrage, surprise, and concern.

"As I said before and as you can plainly see," Anne resumed, "I am not fit to be a wife, let alone mistress of a large estate. Please Mother, on my behalf, do not insist on this."

"But who else will Darcy marry?" Lady Catherine responded in perplexity. So accustomed was she to the idea of uniting the estates of Rosings and Pemberley that she had never contemplated any alternative. The inhabitants of the room could read her next question in her countenance, though it wasn't asked aloud: "Who will marry you, Anne?"

"Let me assure you, ma'am, that I have no desire to marry. I had much rather be allowed to keep quietly to myself here." Anne looked timidly at her mother. It had taken a great bout of courage to defy her and she was nearly drained from the exertion. Noting her fatigue, Lady Catherine's motherly instincts overtook her ambitions.

"I would never insist you do something against your will Anne. You are an adult and I have always treated you as such but, right now, I must insist that you act like one by removing upstairs. I predict you will be unable to join us for dinner following this ridiculous display. You must attend more carefully to your lady, Mrs. Jenkinson."

Anne complied, followed by both the chastened Mrs. Jenkinson and her mother, who sharply ordered the housekeeper to show the guests to their rooms. Both Darcys breathed slight sighs of relief. They would not be thrown from the house that evening.

Anne did not join them for dinner, a quiet affair. Never had the siblings seen their Aunt Catherine so subdued, though she was not so downcast as to deny herself the pleasure of interrogating Georgiana regarding the progress of her studies, but even this was done half-heartedly. Typically Lady Catherine took great pride in Georgiana's achievements. She considered her niece amongst the most accomplished young ladies in the kingdom, in no small part due to her own invaluable advice, but on that night it only served as a reminder of Anne's chronic ill health. The diners did not touch on the subject of marriage, it was still too raw, yet Darcy recognized that it must be resumed before his departure if he was to remain on cordial terms with his aunt.

Upon waking the next morning, Darcy looked out the window to observe that, though the grounds remained wet, the rain had momentarily subsided. He decided to seize the opportunity for some fresh air and called for a mount, hoping the exercise would compose his thoughts. So focused was he on how to resume the previous day's conversation with his aunt that it was not until he passed the parsonage, situated just outside the grounds, that he realized he had unwittingly performed Mr. Collins a second service by not depriving him of the joy, which he was sure to relish, of announcing his impending nuptials to Lady Catherine himself. "Let him enjoy it," he thought while dismounting in order to walk around the house, taking note of its appointments so he could answer any questions the Bennets might have about Mary's new home. It would be far more pleasant when his future trips to Rosings could be conducted in Elizabeth's company; she would delight in the easy access to her sister, just across the park. So be it. Since the night of the assembly, event after event had decidedly proven that fate could be trusted to care for its own concerns. The rectory was well cared for and salubriously situated; he believed Miss Mary would like it very well.

He returned to the house, changed from his muddied clothes, and proceeded downstairs to find Lady Catherine partaking of a solitary breakfast. "Ah, Darcy," was her grim greeting. "You always were an early riser. How do you find the grounds?"

"Lovely even in this foul weather, Aunt."

"Indeed they are," she snapped, wondering in silent bitterness why he would reject an estate he so admired when it was his for the taking, though she well knew the answer. "You might mind the weather and reconsider your impetuous travel arrangements."

Darcy chose not to resume that topic, "When I return in the spring with my cousin Fitzwilliam, ma'am, I will look thoroughly into any repairs that are needed with your steward, as usual. My cursory survey this morning will aid me then. I imagine that the western wall will need to be reinforced if this winter proves difficult."

"Perhaps you would rather forgo the burden. It would befit you to remain in London throughout the season. You shall need to find your-self a bride."

Such a direct attack he could not ignore, "My dear Aunt Catherine, please, let not this sorry business be a source of bitterness between us. You know I shall always care for your affairs. Our family is small and we depend on each other – there lies our strength. A rift would be unbearable. If I choose to add to our numbers I truly hope, as one of my nearest relations, you will welcome her as an asset and love her as a niece. Georgiana, too, someday will marry. This is how we will secure the future, both for ourselves as well as for you and Anne."

Darcy's appeal was well aimed. Lady Catherine, in spite of her imperious demeanor, was rather frightened on the score of familial strength. Her heritage and wealth had always served as a protective force against the ills of life, but she knew as well as anyone that not only money was needed: strength is found in numbers. With Sir Louis de Bourgh long dead and Anne's health uncertain, she faced the very real and terrifying prospect of finding herself left all alone in the world. The appeal of a marriage between Darcy and Anne was not just the union of two great estates but also the security such a match would provide. The insurance of a next generation was all important. She hated the idea of being the last vestige of her line, slowly fizzling out. But Anne was right, as was Darcy. Childbirth could quite possibly kill her daughter, and her nephew would never abandon her interests, no matter who he married. He, Georgiana, and her other nephews could be counted on to do their duty and expand the family. Instinct led her to try and hold her few relatives together in a closely knit group but that course being blocked, she could concede that bringing in new members was a rational strategy to pursue. After mulling over these thoughts she was reassured enough to speak in nearly her usual, officious manner, "Very well then Darcy. I shall leave you to your own affairs. But mind who you do choose as a wife. Don't be swept away by one of these weak, sniveling women who are all the fashion these days. The mistress of Pemberley must have the strength to wield such a household. Had I been raised like one of your modern ladies, this estate would have been in sorry condition indeed when Sir Louis died. Find a wife who is up to the task or mark my words, you will learn to regret it."

Darcy smiled. Clearly, he was forgiven. "You are quite right Aunt," he replied. "London is full of women who may have all the familial credentials but who are, nonetheless, unfit for the task. These fashionable ladies of the Ton may entertain beautifully but it takes more than a well played concerto and drawing room elegance to be mistress of a large estate. I require a wife who will be my partner in improving Pemberley but, sadly, a woman who combines intelligence and grace is a rare gem indeed." He tried not to think of his words as deceitful.

"Do not be so quick to dismiss breeding, Darcy," Lady Catherine said sternly. "Nothing is more important. But perhaps London is not the place for you to search. A gently bred lady of the country might suit, someone uncorrupted by the frivolity of town. I shall keep an eye out for an appropriate candidate: a lady of good but retired family."

"That is an excellent idea Aunt. Just what is wanted."

The remainder of the short visit passed companionably. Georgiana played for the family that evening to everyone's great enjoyment but, in particular, to Anne's. While most ladies would cringe at the idea of spinsterhood, it came to Anne de Bourgh as a great relief that her mother had abandoned her matrimonial schemes. Rarely had she been as relaxed and content as she was that evening, happy in the companionship of her cousins.

Brother and sister departed immediately after Matins, despite Lady Catherine's ongoing protests against traveling in the rain on a Sunday. Just narrowly did they escape Mr. Collins, newly returned from Hertfordshire, as he hastened towards their party upon completion of the service. Darcy wondered briefly how much of his budding relationship with Elizabeth Bennet Mr. Collins would reveal to Lady Catherine but decided he cared not. His aunt had declared her intention of letting him decide for himself and he planned to make her abide by it. The separation from Elizabeth had proven to him the depth of his love for her. He had Georgiana's approval and, in a nominal manner, his aunt's. No rain storm, muddy road, or holy day would prevent him from asking for her hand as soon as possible – Tuesday, at the latest.

Chapter 18

At Longbourn the incessant rain was virtually ignored by the family, fully rapt as they were in the flurry of two weddings to plan. Only Lydia had cause to complain of boredom and was chagrined to find herself ignored by a mother who had no time for such considerations. Jane and Elizabeth were almost never alone as the former's attention was totally occupied between Mrs. Bennet's demands, regarding even the most minute of wedding details, and the devoted Mr. Bingley's daily visits.

This left Elizabeth, when her attention wasn't similarly garnered by her mother, with a great deal of leisure for reflection. The solitude was sorely needed as she had never before had more on which to think. How overwhelming were the changes only a few days could bring! She was to see her dear Jane happily married – who could deserve it more? Remarkably, Mary too would soon be suitably settled in a marriage that would alleviating the long born burden of the entail. And then there was Mr. Darcy – the fine hairs on her arms prickled at the thought of him. At the slightest break in the storm she sought relief outdoors. As the weather confined most of the neighborhood to their homes, no one observed her skipping along the muddy paths, sometimes spinning wildly in a circle, her skirts billowing about her, fluttering just like her uncontainable excitement. Always had she hoped but never allowed herself to truly believe that she would meet exactly the man who, in disposition and talents, would most suit her, let alone one with the means Mr. Darcy had at his disposal! Though she could not visualize the grandeur of Pemberley, she could clearly imagine herself and Mr. Darcy wandering across a magnificent landscape – like those she had seen in her father's lithographs of the Peaks – happy, content, and thoroughly in love. "Stop it!" she admonished herself. It would not do to think on it, not while his intentions were still uncertain. But the overture he had made had already demolished her paltry defenses and she could not prevent herself from dwelling on the many ways in which he so perfectly answered all her wishes. Should he propose, she was determined that all the advantages of the union be not felt on her side alone. No indeed. She would do her utmost to be the best mistress of Pemberley (though she barely dared to think the words) possible. She would relax the master's severe personality as, she was beginning to recognize, only she could. She would attend to the needs of the tenants in the efficient manner of an intelligent and compassionate woman. But then again, should he not propose – well, as that idea had become far too painful to contemplate, it was easily banished.

While Elizabeth struggled, the marriage plans plowed quickly forward around her, overcoming all worries and aggravations in their path. No obstacle could stand up to the combined force of alter bound Bennets. An example of this phenomenon arose when the time for Mr. Collins' departure approached and he made much of delaying the choosing of a date for the wedding until his return in two weeks, it being imperative that he consult with Lady Catherine in order to determine when he could be spared. "I had suspected I'd need be absent from my duties on only one more occasion," he declared with great pomp, "but now I find I must beg my noble patroness' indulgence twice – the first on the day when my union with Miss Mary will render me the happiest of men and the second, when I can perform that same service for my future brother, Mr. Bingley, and my dear cousin Jane."

"But surely," Jane timidly replied, "if your presence is required at Hunsford you need not attend our simple ceremony."

"So kind of you Miss Bennet, to think of the needs of my parish, but not for the world would I miss the opportunity of officiating at your wedding."

As no one had ever requested that Mr. Collins perform such a service, this announcement was grudgingly received. Both Jane and Mr. Bingley felt extremely awkward: they were complacent by nature and did not wish to disappoint Mr. Collins by rejecting his uninvited offer, but they were equally uninclined to listen to his absurd, if well-intended, droning throughout their wedding. It was Mary who offered an acceptable solution to this particular quandary, observing that a double ceremony would display a more befitting appearance of economy while providing the added benefit of allowing Mr. Collins more time for his duties at Hunsford, which Mary intended to encourage him to attend to most assiduously. Though he was unconcerned for economy, Bingley happily accepted this solution to the problem and related the tale with relish to Darcy when he returned to Netherfield on Monday evening.

"Narrow escape there, hey Darcy? Imagine the happiest moment of my life being presided over by Mr. Collins!"

"Frightening indeed. Are you truly as happy as you appear Bingley? Such animation as you display this evening is unusual even by your standards."

"Yes I am. No one could be happier." He grew serious, "Jane is the most wonderful woman the world could possibly contain and I could not be more honored that she has accepted my hand." Both gentlemen quietly sipped their brandy. "And what of you Darcy?" Bingley broke the silence.

"Me, Bingley?"

"Yes, you Darcy. How are your feelings towards Miss Elizabeth proceeding?"

"I thought of little else while away."

"And?" Bingley prodded expectantly.

Darcy suppressed a smile and said, with his customary sobriety, "I look forward to being in her company again."

"Is that all?" Bingley asked, somewhat crestfallen. "I assured Jane that you would be ready to propose upon your return."

"I'm not sure what compelled you to make such an assertion. Not everyone need run into marriage in your head long manner, Bingley." That gentleman happily laughed off the jab.

"What of Wickham?" Darcy changed the topic. "Have you seen any more of him?"

"Not at all. Caroline seems to have relinquished her defense of the acquaintance, thankfully. In fact, I believe her largely returned to her normal self."

"Glad to hear it Bingley. It was rather painful being in her company while she insisted on glaring at me so."

"Yes, I too shall not miss her glowering across the table from me everyday, not that her smiles are all that much more comforting," he smirked. "You will accompany me when I visit Longbourn tomorrow, will you not?"

Darcy adamantly agreed that he would.

Thrilled that the rain had finally ceased and anxious to be out and about, Lydia and Kitty set forth the following morning on a walk to Meryton. The excitement of being released from the house was compounded by the announcement just made that Mr. Bingley intended to give a Christmas ball, both in honor of the holiday and to celebrate his impending marriage. This gave added direction to the girls walk, as they were determined to survey every inch of available merchandise the town had to offer in their quest for the perfect ribbons and trims for the event. It was imperative that this task be completed expediently so they would have ample time to write to their Aunt Gardiner, requesting any missing items be brought from London when she visited. Merry they certainly were with the added felicity of a ball to anticipate on top of all the other excitement currently found at Longbourn.

"If Aunt and Uncle Gardiner would be so obliging, I'm sure I'd just adore shoe-roses from London!" Lydia enthusiastically exclaimed.

"Lizzy suggests Aunt Gardiner would not wish to be burdened with such trivialities," Kitty giggled, "though I'm certain she plans to request a whole medley of items for herself, anxious as she must be to please Mr. Darcy."

"If Mr. Darcy should marry Lizzy," Lydia mused aloud, "do you think he might be induced to give a ball in our honor, in order to properly introduce us to London society? Certainly he must already be planning a season for Miss Darcy and it would be easy enough to include us in the festivities."

"Oh! I cannot imagine so. It would be too great an imposition, would it not?

"How could it be? The few pounds we would cost him mean nothing to a man like Mr. Darcy."

"What do you think she will be like, Lydia?"

"Whoever do you mean?"

"Why Georgiana Darcy of course." Kitty had been consumed with curiosity regarding this young lady ever since she had first been made aware of her existence, creating quite a fantastic portrait in her mind of a lady combining all that amounts to perfection: talent, grace, and carriage. It was an image greatly enhanced by the glowing accounts she had heard Miss Bingley provide of Miss Darcy.

"How am I to know what she is like? Hopefully we will find her more sociable than her brother!" Lydia carelessly retorted.

"I like Mr. Darcy – so handsome and mysterious! I imagine his sister must be terribly refined," Kitty confessed with a hint of nervousness. To herself she thought, "Perhaps once we have been in school for a while she will not find our company too intolerable."

"Well, if Mr. Darcy never manages to propose, we may never even meet her."

"Surely he will propose Lydia, else he would not bestow such attentions on Lizzy – not a gentleman like him!"

"Mr. Bingley and Mr. Collins managed well enough, why should Mr. Darcy hesitate?"

"The comparison is unfair! Mr. Darcy is worlds more refined than Mr. Collins and even quite a bit more so than Mr. Bingley!" Again, the elder sister left much unsaid. She had her own theory as to why Mr. Darcy might hesitate to unite himself to the Bennet family and it was too painful to acknowledge aloud, especially just to be lightly dismissed by Lydia. From their first encounters she had noted the way in which Mr. Darcy observed their behavior with disdain, causing her, for the first time in her life, to critique her own disposition. With her findings she was not content. Kitty already knew she had a tendency towards peevishness (Lizzy having frequently told her so) which she was endeavoring to correct, but now she also recognized that the exuberance which both she and Lydia had often displayed in public, while most effective in garnering the attention of the local gentlemen, might not be perceived as terribly becoming in a young lady. Whenever Mr. Darcy was around she had taken to watching his responses and checking herself accordingly, that gentleman holding as elevated a place in her mind as his sister.

"However will Mary manage to look the bride next to Jane I wonder?" Lydia, in her typical fashion, jumped to a new topic of conversation, never willing to discuss any subject, except finery and gentleman, at any length.

Kitty was happy to think on lighter subjects and responded, "If Mama has her way, with a great deal too much lace!" Both girls laughed heartily.

"When I marry I mean to have a far more fashionable gown than those our sisters have chosen. Surely something from Paris! I wonder what Lizzy will wear when she marries Mr. Darcy? That will surely be a grand affair."

"By your own admission, do you not mean if she marries Mr. Darcy?"

"Oh not again Kitty! It is all far too tiresome!" Lydia sighed. "When we are in school I imagine the Darcy connection will be of great advantage in establishing our position socially. Oh, I do hope that Papa chooses the school in Bath! What fun we should have with so many balls and such a continuous supply of new gentlemen to meet!"

"Look Lydia," Kitty pointed ahead of her as they drew near the town, "is that not Miss Bingley?"

Indeed it was Miss Bingley, walking along the opposite side of the road, totally oblivious to the Bennet sisters and entirely engrossed by her escort – none other than Mr. Wickham.

Lydia called out a cheerful greeting before Kitty could prevent her. Miss Bingley started and looked up, staring for a moment without a hint of recognition. Finally she recovered and nodded the briefest of acknowledgments before proceeding on her way. Mr. Wickham bowed handsomely and followed her.

"Why must Wickham be the most handsome of all the officers!" Lydia lamented, swooning slightly at his gallantry. "If only Papa were not so stubbornly set against him! Surely he would find my company to be far more amiable than that of the stuffy Miss Bingley!"

"Mr. Darcy calls him a thorough scoundrel, Lydia. His company should not be lamented."

"Really Kitty! You almost sound like Lizzy, or even Mary!"

Kitty ignored the taunt. "Perhaps we should inform Papa that we saw them together. Mr. Bingley would certainly disapprove of the association."

"I am sure Miss Bingley knows what she is about," Lydia declared with a dismissive wave of the hand. "Oh Kitty! Just look at that bonnet!"

Distracted by merchandise the girls dropped the subject altogether, never to resume it. After a very pleasant day of shopping and visiting they returned home prepared to pen requests to their Aunt Gardiner for all the items they were happily unable to find, regale their mother with all the gossip gleaned from their Aunt Phillips, and continue to rejoice in all the wedding plans and other excitements that had of late filled their happy world. Mr. Wickham and Miss Bingley were long forgotten.

Chapter 19

An unforeseen benefit, from Elizabeth's perspective, of Mary's time being almost entirely consumed with wedding details was that the pianoforte was uncommonly available. This was particularly fortunate as the distraction of her much neglected practice helped Elizabeth to keep from dwelling on the turmoil of her emotions regarding Mr. Darcy. That morning she had been playing with unaccustomed diligence for several hours, much longer than she had ever been previously known to attend to her music, and so lost in her thoughts was she that she did not perceive the noise accompanying the arrival of the gentlemen from Netherfield. Thus Mr. Darcy was able to stand in the doorway, Elizabeth completely unaware of his presence, and observe her as she played.

Could she have seen him, she would have noted the slight smile that graced his handsome face as he leaned in the doorway and wondered what it portended. He would never have admitted, not at such an early stage of their relationship, to imagining Elizabeth, in clear transposition, gracing Pemberley with her lovely presence. He envisioned her with Georgiana, spending countless hours together in the fine music room, with its beautiful view of the grounds, sharing and relishing each others accomplishments while bonding together in sisterly affection. He wanted this daydream to become reality so badly it manifested itself as a physical ache. Any lingering hesitation he might still have been harboring regarding the action he was about to take was fully vanquished by this felicitous image.

"That was remarkably lovely," he said when she paused. She started slightly at the sound of his voice but, though overcome by a delightful anticipation, did not turn round to greet the intruder. To do so would be to expose the blush that currently warmed her cheeks. She knew not how welcome the sight would have been.

"And who is this who comes upon me so suddenly?" she teased and resumed her performance, now playing softly so that conversation could easily continue. "It surely does not sound like one of my sisters."

"No, I must admit it is not one of your sisters, unless one is so unfortunate as to suffer from a terribly calamity of the throat," he tossed back. "How does this woman do this to me?" he wondered at his own merriment.

Elizabeth laughed, stopped playing, and turned to greet him, her skin now its customary shade, with a brilliant smile that made his heart leap. "Mr. Darcy, you have returned. Welcome back to Hertforshire sir. I trust your travels went well?" She gestured towards a chair in which he happily settled himself.

"My trip to Rosings, though encompassed by rain, was most successful. My aunt, Lady Catherine, finds herself resigned that I shall never be more than her nephew and commands me forthwith to find a hale and hearty wife."

It was no use. She was once again in full blush and had no means to hide it but to stare down at her hands, furtively folded in her lap. How to respond? "That is felicitous," she nervously replied. Darcy, as usual, found delight in her discomfort. Though he had no cruel desire to needlessly torment her, he was thrilled with his ability to render the quick witted woman he loved speechless. Nevertheless, in all their interaction they had been direct with each other – it was what marked their intercourse as unique – and he had every intention of continuing the trend at this most important moment.

"Miss Elizabeth," he began, suddenly feeling rather nervous himself, "I found that you were constantly in my thoughts during my absence. I cannot express the pleasure it is to once again be in your company." He paused, losing his equilibrium in her expectant look.

"Drat!" he thought, rising from his chair to pace the room. This was not how he intended to proceed but, now the moment was upon him, he was suddenly at a loss for words. Elizabeth watched him with concern. He had seemed on the precipice of making the longed for offer of marriage but his current behavior, restless and agitated, did not seem to portend a declaration of love. She braced herself against the rising surge of disappointment and was thereby taken off guard by the simple speech that followed.

"Miss Elizabeth," he began again, finally standing still and gazing at her with an intense look, "forgive my fumbling manner. Typically I am a methodical man but I find to my dismay that method has no place here. I believe you are the woman who would most suit me in life. Will you please do me the very great honor of accepting my hand in marriage?"

The proposal was thus plainly stated. Darcy could not employ the flourishes usually deemed appropriate on such an occasion, but his eyes expressed emotions that no words could ever do justice to. Elizabeth heard in that gaze the most passionate declaration of love and returned it with a warm, comforting, and brilliant smile that clearly conveyed her response. He would never forget the intonation of the nine words she spoke – for the remainder of his life he could clearly recall them and the surge of nourishment they provided his heart, so long neglected: "Of course Mr. Darcy. The honor is all mine."

❧

"Excuse me, sir. May I have word?"

Darcy he was so excited he could barely modulate his voice. Mr. Bennet had to scold a smile from appearing, "Mr. Darcy, of course. Do sit down."

He sat in the same seat he occupied during his last interview with Mr. Bennet, who correctly imagined this man he was about to welcome into the family as the type who would always sit in the same place and indeed, over the years, the leather chair came to be regarded as Mr. Darcy's own whenever he visited Longbourn.

"You can have little doubt what it is I wish to discuss with you, Mr. Bennet," Darcy commenced.

"Indeed?" was the reply, made with a raised brow and a familiar twinkle of the eye.

Mr. Darcy had been well schooled as of late in how to parry with a Bennet. He knew this man was toying with him and spontaneously decided, driven on by his high spirits, to enact a bit of playful revenge. "Yes sir. You are well aware of my attachment to your daughter. She has, this morning, accepted my offer of marriage. I ask, Mr. Bennet, for you to favor our union with your blessing. I promise I will strive to make Miss Kitty the happiest of women."

Mr. Bennet, who had maintained a rather self-satisfied air though the majority of this declaration, turned rather red at its conclusion. His first impulse was to dive across the desk and attempt to throttle the younger (and taller) man who sat across from him, but upon noticing the broad smile on Mr. Darcy's face, he realized the joke was on him. Chuckling, he shook his head, "Pray, what would you do sir, should I hold you to that offer? Life at the mercy of my most fanciful of daughters would be appropriate punishment for the shock you just gave me. I presume you meant to offer for my Lizzy and that it is she who accepted your proposal today?"

"You are correct, Mr. Bennet."

"Very good. Of course you have my blessing. You really needn't have bothered with this quaint ritual of asking my permission when well you know Mrs. Bennet would make my life miserable should I say no."

"Thank you, Mr. Bennet," Darcy said sincerely. Mr. Bennet rose to shake his preferred hand. "This is the greatest honor of my life."

"You deserve her son. Off with you to Elizabeth now." Mr. Bennet was left alone in his library to privately mourn the loss of his most precious child, finding great consolation in the acquisition of such a son-in-law.

❧

"Oh, Mr. Bennet! Our Lizzy, mistress of Pemberley! Just think of it! Mr. Darcy is undoubtedly the most handsome man imaginable. Did you witness him kiss my hand so gallantly? I haven't blushed so fiercely since I was a girl! I must go into Meryton at once and tell my sister Phillips! Call for the carriage, Mr. Bennet. I must have the horses!"

"Slow down Mrs. Bennet so that we may understand one another. What is all this about Lizzy? Mr. Darcy never spoke of Lizzy."

"Never spoke to you … Mr. Bennet, do be serious."

"I am perfectly serious. Mr. Darcy did come and speak with me today but regarding Catherine, not Elizabeth."

"What on Earth has this to do with Kitty?"

"Why, Mr. Darcy intends to marry her of course."

"Marry Kitty! You are just trying to vex me, Mr. Bennet."

"Perhaps, but it was certainly Kitty of whom Mr. Darcy spoke."

"Kitty? Kitty?! KITTY!" Mrs. Bennet screeched as she hurried out the door. Mr. Bennet intercepted her just in time to prevent her from wrecking havoc throughout the household with her faulty information. He confessed his deception to his chagrined wife, but she made only quick mention of her fragile nerves before recovering her happy exclamations over Lizzy's good fortune. That her daughter should make the finest match of anyone in her acquaintance! Mr. Bennet recognized the cruelty of playing such a trick on his wife but, as there was no harm done, he felt he deserved his share in the joke. He chuckled contentedly to himself as his wife bustled back out of the room, eager to attend to the happy couple.

At this juncture, reader dear, I fear I'm in a bit of a quandary regarding what to share with you. I could regale you with a detailed account of the first kiss that was, presumably, shared at some point between our hero and heroine during the course of their courtship, but to do so, as I'm sure you'll agree, would be an unforgivable intrusion on their privacy. Alternatively, I could provide a day to day account of events as they transpired at Longbourn – detailing all the many wedding preparations, the attending squabbles over yards of lace, and the arrangements that Lydia and Kitty enthusiastically made for their upcoming departure to a very respectable educational facility in Bath – but these occurrences are too mundane to require elaboration. So instead I'll just assure you that everything proceeded with as much calm as can be expected, in a household such as Longbourn, between this time and the arrival of the Gardiners for their Christmas visit, but for two notable exceptions. For a proper rendering of the first, we must temporarily leave behind our friends in Hertfordshire and away to Kent.

Chapter 20

With conflicting emotions had Lady Catherine awaited the letter she finally received from her nephew, a full three days overdue by the great lady's estimation. Its contents were as follows:

Netherfield Hall, Hertfordshire, 27 Nov.

My Dearest Aunt,

I am returned to Mr. Bingley's home after an uneventful, if muddy, ride to London from Netherfield. Both Georgiana and I thoroughly enjoyed our visit. I can only apologize again for both its spontaneity and brevity but, as I am sure you are now fully aware thanks to the intelligence which Mr. Collins undoubtedly provided you, I had pressing matters to attend to here.

Forgive me, Aunt Catherine, for not being more forthcoming with you, but I am afraid I was not certain of either my heart or my course of action until lately. It was my conversations with you and Georgiana that revealed my true feelings on the matter. Your words particularly directed me, as they had the wisdom of experience. When you charged me to find a strong, capable wife, untainted by societal affectations, I had no doubt that you would approve of my choice.

Miss Elizabeth Bennet has all the ability and elegance one could ask for in a mistress of Pemberley. You are familiar with the circumstances of the family and, particularly, the Longbourn estate – it has been the seat of the Bennets for generations. You performed an act of immeasurable kindness when you directed Mr. Collins to seek a bride amongst his cousins. A tragedy has been thwarted and an old and noble estate will not be deprived of its rightful lineage. I can also assure you that you will find Mary Bennet to be a most advantageous match for Mr. Collins – I only refrained from doing so earlier so as not to deprive him of the joy of announcing his good fortune to you himself.

Miss Elizabeth Bennet has little personal portion but I find I am glad of it. Had it not been for needful and honorable economy she would surely have been far more exposed to the exact society against which you warned me, potentially having lost the sincerity and goodness that so mark her: values that form the backbone of England's honored country gentry.

I must admit, dear Aunt, that I am not looking forward to calling Mr. Collins Brother. I am sure he is an admirable rector, but I find his obsequiousness quite overwhelming. Yet I have great hopes that Miss Mary will improve him immeasurably, especially with the benefit of your example and guidance.

Miss Elizabeth and I plan to marry at Pemberley in the new year, on Thursday, the 9th of January. I know this is a far from ideal time of year for travel northwards, but I hope you and Anne will be able to attend nonetheless. Please relay my best wishes to my dear cousin. May God bless you both.

Your loving nephew,
Fitzwilliam Darcy

Lady Catherine was surprised, having commenced reading in high dudgeon, to feel as mollified as she did upon finishing the letter. Darcy and Georgiana had just pulled away from the church when Mr. Collins began lamenting that he had not had the opportunity to assure Mr. Darcy of one Miss Elizabeth Bennet's good health before his departure. Mere minutes extracted the entire story from Mr. Collins, rendering Lady Catherine extremely indignant ever since. This long awaited missive was perused with great interest and attention.

Darcy and she agreed on one point: Lady Catherine did not relish the notion of a familial connection to Mr. Collins. She had selected him to serve as her rector, not her relative, and her requirements for those two distinct roles could not be more different. In just the few short days since his return to Hunsford, she believed she could detect in him an increased air of importance, which she thought thoroughly unbecoming, attributing it to his presumed relationship with her own nephew. Granted, she would have been equally annoyed if he had failed to ascribe the appropriate value to such a potential relation and the honor thus conveyed. Some solace she found in Darcy's assurance that this Mary Bennet was a girl of some sense – she would perhaps prove a valuable companion to Anne – but the future Mrs. Darcy she could only regard with distrust.

Unable to refute the advice she herself had provided her nephew, Lady Catherine could, nevertheless, dispute his interpretation of it. Her mind eagerly grasped for some logical ground upon which to object to the marriage. The idea of Fitzwilliam Darcy of Pemberley connecting himself to a girl of no fortune was galling, an anathema to everything she valued. Unfortunately, as was made evident by his letter, arguments founded in status and wealth would not suffice to sway Darcy. Having never met the girl, what other means could she utilize in dissuading her nephew? "Well," she decided, "that is a matter I certainly do have the power to rectify." She would travel to Hertfordshire and see the lady for herself. Soon too, before the engagement was formally announced. Knowing full well that once the news became known every person in England of note would be speaking of little else than Fitzwilliam Darcy's astounding proposal to an unknown country miss, she wasted no time in her purpose. Gathering her writing materials, Lady Catherine penned the following letter:

Rosings Park, 29 Nov.

Dear Nephew,

I cannot express how shocked I am by the contents of your letter. Mr. Collins did indeed mention a presumed attachment between yourself and the sister of his betrothed but never had I believed the thing should be settled to abruptly. Perhaps you are behaving precipitously – how long have you even known the lady? It falls upon me, nearly your closest relation, to advise you in this, the most critical decision of your life. To this end, I will depart for Hertfordshire tomorrow, stopping one night in London. Please advise Mr. Bingley that he may expect me Tuesday, between noon and one o'clock. I shall remain at Netherfield only long enough to insure that you have not made a grave mistake in your selection of a bride. As you are so sure of your choice, you may advise Mr. Bingley that he should not be imposed upon for long.

Your affectionate aunt,

Lady Catherine de Bourgh

❧

"Good Lord," Darcy moaned as he read his aunt's missive at breakfast the following Monday.

"Bad news Darcy?" Bingley inquired nonchalantly. When he received no response his concern became genuine. "Darcy?"

He was not pleased to have to inform Bingley of his aunt's impending intrusion, though he was thankful she had at least regarded him the civility, so recently overlooked by himself, of providing notice, though it be short. He had twenty-four hours to prepare for her arrival, no extra time to lose.

Miss Bingley and Mrs. Hurst joined them in the breakfast parlor before he had responded to his friend. Following the obligatory civilities he immediately made his announcement.

"It is fortunate you are all here," he began, not bothering to consider Mr. Hurst's absence, "for I have a rather unusual request to make. It seems my aunt, Lady Catherine de Bourgh, has some urgent business about which she wishes to speak to me and has already departed from Rosings. She expects to be welcomed by you as a guest tomorrow."

Mrs. Hurst glanced at her sister in astonishment but received only a smirk in reply. Clearly Caroline presumed she had a very good idea what business brought Lady Catherine to Netherfield and found amusement in the scenario. Looking instead to her brother, who also correctly guessed Lady Catherine's intentions, Louisa saw his agitation. Her siblings' differing reactions left Mrs. Hurst with a confounding sense of foreboding.

"Of course she will be most welcome," Miss Bingley quickly chimed in before Mr. Darcy could continue. "It will be an honor to host such an illustrious guest."

"Yes Darcy," Mr. Bingley seconded, "of course any connection of yours will always be welcome in my home."

"Thank you," Mr. Darcy replied to both sister and brother. "I sincerely apologize for any inconvenience you may incur on my aunt's behalf. She says she will arrive between noon and one. Knowing my aunt, that might possibly mean eleven.

"I shall make the arrangements with the housekeeper at once," Miss Bingley excused herself and exited the room. She did as she said, making sure every proper detail was attended to, but following that task she also informed another individual of the expected visitor, for reasons having little to do with hospitality.

"I intend to leave for Longbourn immediately," Darcy said tersely as he rose. Dryly he continued, "I have a feeling the Bennets also need time to prepare for the unsolicited honor they shall so soon be receiving."

"I shall accompany you," Bingley replied. They bade Mrs. Hurst good morning and left the room, where she continued to contemplate her breakfast alone, wondering what worse Lady Catherine's visit could portend than a hastily broken engagement.

"So Lady Catherine is interested in meeting your fiancée?" Bingley asked in the hall. Darcy nodded. "I thought that might be at the root of this. Very well then. Let us be on our way." They were in the saddle before the hour had elapsed.

Elizabeth and Jane were surprised to see their intendeds riding towards the house. They were not expected until much later, when they were to collect a small party of Bennets and escort them to Netherfield to dine. Now that Miss Bingley had ceased sulking about the house, Bingley felt it was well past time for him to repay all the hospitality he had been enjoying at Longbourn. Accordingly, the two eldest daughters and their parents had received invitations in Caroline's own hand. Thus this unexpected arrival left the ladies rather perplexed. Jane smoothed her gown, wishing she had taken greater care with her toilet, while Elizabeth wondered what could possibly be amiss.

Despite the puzzlement of the ladies, the gentlemen received what had become their customary warm welcomes. Mr. Bingley joined Jane on the grounds while Mr. Darcy, having expressed to Elizabeth that he had something to announce to the entire family, was shown into the house. Mrs. Bennet only momentarily fussed over Mr. Darcy upon his entrance into the sitting room, having now become practiced at curbing her effusions in his company. Kitty and Lydia seemed pleasantly occupied contriving their new school wardrobes and the distant tones of the surprisingly lighthearted piece Mary was practicing softly enveloped the parlor. Mr. Darcy smiled on the scene. Perhaps there was reason to hope that Lady Catherine's visit would go smoothly.

"Please excuse our unexpected call this morning, but I have received news of some import which I felt should be shared promptly. My aunt, Lady Catherine, arrives at Netherfield tomorrow morning and I know she will be most anxious to make your acquaintance."

"Lady Catherine de Bourgh!" Mrs. Bennet squealed in much her typical fashion, loud enough that Mary apparently could hear her, that young lady having ceased to play. Darcy cringed at the shrill sound and feared he had been precipitous in his optimism, but Mrs. Bennet was quick to remember herself and checked her enthusiasm. With renewed composure, she happily bustled off to converse with Hill about fish and pheasant, just in case the great lady might be persuaded to join them for dinner. Kitty was frozen in frightened astonishment while Lydia went about her business, as unconcerned as if she routinely visited and entertained such distinguished personages.

"Lady Catherine is coming here?" Elizabeth reiterated, as if to confirm the truth of her fiancé's words. She had grown a bit pale but her chin determinedly high. The news chagrined her. She could not feel appreciative of such an obvious intrusion into her affairs by a stranger but, simultaneously, in spite of her pride, she desperately desired this particular lady's approval. Perceiving her discomfiture, Darcy sat down in the chair beside her, taking her hand comfortingly.

"She wants to meet you and, I am afraid that judging by the tone of her letter, she may be seeking to criticize. But I assure you she shall find nothing to complain of. How could she?"

Elizabeth looked up at Darcy gratefully. Gazing into her eyes, she felt no doubt as to the truth of his words.

"Excuse me," Mary said from the doorway, "but has something occurred regarding Lady Catherine de Bourgh? I just heard my mother cry her name in a quite disturbing fashion."

Darcy reluctantly released Elizabeth's hand, rose, and walked towards Mary. "You heard correctly, Miss Mary, though let me assure you that nothing untoward has happened. My aunt intends to visit Netherfield for a few days this week and wishes to be introduced at Longbourn."

To his surprise, Darcy observed Mary's chin tilt upwards in an identical manner to Elizabeth's and it occurred to him, in a sudden bout of sympathy, just how much heavier such news would fall on her than on his betrothed. Mary would not be meeting a new relation but her new benefactress, a woman's whose goodwill was essential to her future. Elizabeth would surely benefit from Lady Catherine's approval but it was not vital to her happiness; no one would now dissuade Darcy from his chosen course. He was impressed by his future sister's fortitude. Mary simply asked when the honor was to be expected. Mr. Darcy repeated what details he had but was unable to confirm when a visit to Longbourn would take place, though he imagined it would be on the morrow.

"Oh Mr. Darcy!" Kitty suddenly exclaimed. "Whatever shall Lady Catherine think of us? Never have I met anyone so grand. Need we wear full dress?"

"Don't be absurd Kitty," Elizabeth responded on his behalf, distracted by her own concerns. "Lady Catherine would surely not appreciate it should we put on a display for her sake. Certainly, with Mr. Collins as a rector, she knows something of our circumstances. Typical morning dress will be perfectly sufficient."

Mr. Darcy noticed Kitty's face fall and felt moved to reassure her. "I believe, Miss Kitty, that you have a blue muslin that is quite becoming on you. Something of that sort would be most appropriate."

Kitty blushed joyfully at such a demonstration of attention from Mr. Darcy. "Oh thank you sir!" she exclaimed. "If you will excuse me, I shall go right away and make sure it is presentable."

Lydia rolled her eyes but followed her sister out of the room. Darcy, Elizabeth, and even Mary shared an amused glance before bursting into laughter. "You have certainly made quite an impression on my sister, Mr. Darcy," Elizabeth teased, her good humor, as usual, overriding her anxiety. "Need I be jealous?"

"Certainly not," Mr. Darcy replied, straightening into his most distinguished posture.

"But I hear so much of your admiration for Kitty. My father said you ardently declared so much in his library." Darcy was speechless.

"If you will both excuse me," Mary said stiffly, experiencing the awkwardness of an intruder. "I shall return to my music."

The couple watched her depart, her back rigidly straight. They stood in thoughtful silence for a moment before Darcy regained Elizabeth's hand. "I was only avenging myself on your father," he explained almost sheepishly.

"And he thoroughly enjoyed the joke, I assure you."

"My aunt will like Miss Mary."

"And you take it for granted that your aunt will approve of me?" Elizabeth asked with quiet, assumed bravado.

Darcy, always astounded when this confident woman betrayed any timidity, smiled at her warmly. "She would certainly be a fool not to," he reassured her.

"And what of Mama? Can we expect Lady Catherine to find her barely restrained tongue charming as opposed to shockingly vulgar?"

"You are harsh on your mother."

She stared at him skeptically.

"She may, at times," he cleared his throat, "betray a bit of over enthusiasm, especially where her daughters are concerned, but her heart is almost always in the right place. It is only natural that she should rejoice in her family's good fortune."

"And you believe your aunt will view her so charitably?"

"I believe we have more to fear from my aunt's manners than your mother's. Mrs. Bennet will likely be a bit awed by Lady Catherine while Lady Catherine, quite secure in her position, can be depended upon to be overly condescending, as demonstrated in the ease with which she has invited herself to Netherfield." He frowned, "I do hope she will be gracious."

"You think she is inclined to make things difficult for us?" Elizabeth asked, the concern returned to her voice.

"I shall be with you. If she insults you or your family, she insults me as well. I will not stand for it."

She tucked her arm into his and smiled up at him with the familiar twinkle of amusement in her eyes. "What a formidable man you are, Mr. Darcy. You have weathered my interrogation admirably. I can only pity the person who attempts to thwart you."

"Save your pity for me, my dear Miss Elizabeth. I assure you I shall require it far more than my aunt before this week has passed."

Chapter 21

As Elizabeth dressed for dinner a knock on the door announced Mary, come to assist in her preparations. This surprised Elizabeth, such an offer having rarely been extended from her younger sister before, but she happily accepted. After helping her to don her gown and fix her hair, Mary complimented the effect. Now Elizabeth was certain her sister was perturbed, Mary not being one to promote vanity. As was her custom, she dove right into the heart of the matter, "Mary, are you nervous about Lady Catherine's visit?"

"No. Not precisely nervous," was the reply. "I am well aware that Lady Catherine is not venturing here to meet her rector's intended. It is you she comes to see."

"But surely she will be interested in you as well."

"Yes. I imagine so," she paused. "From what I have gathered from Mr. Collins' discourse on his patroness, Lady Catherine takes great interest in even the most minute details of people's lives. I believe she will ask many forward questions."

"That certainly concurs with Mr. Darcy's description of his aunt. It seems she is very enthusiastic in the management of affairs, be they hers or not."

"All I need do is respond properly."

"Yes, I imagine you will handle examination much more patiently than I." Mary looked down. "What is the matter Mary? Surely there is something more on your mind?"

Mary took a deep breath, "You will attempt not to antagonize her, will you Lizzy?"

"Antagonize her! Why would I wish to do such a thing?"

"Not purposefully, of course. But you know as well as I that your pride sometimes could be interpreted as impertinence. Surely not all great people can be believed to find it as charming as Mr. Darcy. It is unbecoming for a young lady to speak too freely with their elders."

"Odd how you do not follow your own dictum," Elizabeth chided. Mary blushed and stared down at clutched hands, causing her sister to repent her harsh tongue. "You fear Mr. Collins will suffer should Lady Catherine find me unacceptable." Mary didn't respond but the firm, remotely pained look in her eyes told Elizabeth all she needed to know.

She sighed and arranged the finishing touches to her dress. "I shall be on my best behavior, I promise. I do not desire to incur the lady's wrath anymore than you. In fact, I am most anxious to gain her approval, as you should certainly realize."

"Thank you Lizzy," was Mary's quiet reply before quickly exiting the room. Elizabeth was left to contemplate whether her sister would ever be able to perceive her own faults as well as she detected those of others.

Elizabeth managed to relay the content of this conversation to Mr. Darcy through the course of the evening, though frequently interrupted by Mrs. Bennet's chatter and Miss Bingley's cold civilities. Mary's concerns, though annoying, had renewed her own. Darcy did everything he could to reassure her while Miss Bingley, from across the room, watched the couple's tender exchanges. Mrs. Hurst could detect a gleam of menace in her sister's eyes.

Lady Catherine de Bourgh arrived just after noon the following day. Never one to proceed in a manner less than what was do to her grandeur, her ladyship's coach and four bore a retinue of servants for Miss Bingley to assiduously attend to, happy to be housing such fine equipage. She personally escorted Lady Catherine to the best guest quarters and oversaw the staff as they attended to every one of her many needs. Caroline took pride in the perfect grace which her expensive education had supplied her, glorying in her assurance that such a demonstration of her accomplishments could only enhance the disparity Lady Catherine would observe, when at Longbourn, between town refinement and country manners.

How sad that such effort was wasted! Lady Catherine had never heard of Miss Caroline Bingley (Darcy never having mentioned the existence of such a person, as he surely would were she worth notice) so assumed her an inferior specimen of womanhood immediately upon introduction. Still the great lady was pleased by her reception, Darcy having expressed what she considered a most appropriate degree of delight at seeing her, his apparent ease relieving some of her concern over his intended match. Had he seemed nervous and concerned for her disapproval, she would have been immediately convinced that matters were not well. Instead, as he happily spoke to her of the Bennet family, displaying not a hint of the anxiety he felt, Lady Catherine found herself eagerly anticipating honoring the quaint estate her nephew described with a visit. She was not fatigued after her journey: would not hear of resting. She intended to meet the

Bennets at once. Thus, as predicted, mere hours after her arrival Lady
Catherine, Mr. Darcy, and Mr. Bingley were comfortably ensconced
in the Netherfield carriage and on the road to Longbourn.

Kitty and Lydia, having been employed as lookouts, resoundingly
sounded the alarm at first sight of the carriage. The family assembled
in the sitting room, perfectly primped and equipped with the items
they had predetermined to pursue. Mr. Bennet had gone so far as to
choose several books to move from his library to the parlor, where he
never read, so he could be seen to be doing so amongst his family. He
smiled at the ladies as they diligently pursued their work. If they were
always so intently distracted as they now appeared, perhaps the room
would be a pleasant place to indulge his favorite hobby. Mrs. Hill,
wearing her best apron, announced Lady Catherine de Bourgh with as
much flourish as she could muster, fully relishing the honor of such a
fine guest. Lady Catherine, as always, approved of such deference to
her consequence and entered the room with a mind to be pleased.

Mr. Darcy began the introductions. Mrs. Bennet, even more flattered
than Hill to be receiving a guest of such high importance, was perfect in
her politeness. Lady Catherine, in turn, perceived the sardonic twinkle
in Mr. Bennet's eye and instantly deemed him the model country squire,
in the happy state of needing improvement and able to greatly benefit
from her advice. A beaming Mr. Bingley proudly presented Jane, whose
serene beauty and calm manner always pleased everyone.

"And this is Miss Elizabeth Bennet, Aunt." Darcy continued, "Miss
Elizabeth, it is my pleasure to present my aunt, Lady Catherine de
Bourgh."

"Welcome to Longbourn, your Ladyship. It is an honor to make your acquaintance."

Lady Catherine surveyed the young woman in front of her, head held high, eyes bright and sparkling (much like her father's), and found herself intrigued by the odd little woman. Pretty, in a way, but certainly not a remarkable beauty, nothing compared to her sister. "Miss Elizabeth, I have been most interested in meeting you. My nephew informs me that congratulations are in order."

"Yes indeed, ma'am. Please allow me to assure you that I never dreamed to be so fortunate as to gain the affections of such an honorable man as Mr. Darcy."

She watched as Elizabeth's eyes met Darcy's and was astonished at the sight of her severe nephew's grin. "He is entranced," she thought, continuing to observe the couple, "but this Miss Elizabeth is no coquette. Very well, let it be a love match. He could certainly have done worse. By the looks of that Miss Bingley, she would have liked to have gotten her claws into him. Imagine, a creature like that! Oh no. Miss Elizabeth Bennet so be it."

"May I present my sister, Mary Bennet."

Both girls were dark, in contrast to the eldest, but Lady Catherine would never have guessed these two to be sisters. As forward and joyful as Elizabeth was, Mary seemed equally demure and reserved, though not shy. She curtsied and waited very properly for Lady Catherine's notice, a noticeable tilt of determination in her upturned chin. "Then again," wondered Lady Catherine, "maybe there is more to the future Mrs. Collins."

"Miss Mary Bennet, Mr. Collins has told me much about you. I suggested he choose a wife amongst his cousins at Longbourn and I am pleased he has heeded my advice."

"Thank you, Lady Catherine. I am honored by your interest and, as you well know, Mr. Collins treasures all your suggestions."

"Indeed he does child! He will be pleased you remembered to remind me," Lady Catherine acknowledged with the barest hint of an amused smile. To herself she said, "Yes, Miss Mary has her wits about her. Very good. Perhaps she will make something out of that goose Collins."

Kitty and Lydia were presented in turn but remained so very quiet and demur, awed as even the latter was by the quality of Lady Catherine's gown, that her ladyship happily assumed they were not yet out, a misconception no one bothered to correct.

"You say you are fortunate to have gained my nephew's affections, Miss Elizabeth, but I wonder if you fully appreciate the illustrious line into which you intend to marry. Fitzwilliam Darcy is the living embodiment of two noble houses; the lady who shall bear his name must be worthy of such an honor."

Elizabeth raised a brow, shared a glance with Darcy, and smiled becomingly at Lady Catherine in response, deciding she had best not share her present thoughts.

"Your estate, Mr. Bennet, is pleasant, though this sitting room must be uncomfortable in the summer. Have you ever considered improvements?"

"Not since I married Mrs. Bennet."

"That is as it should be. My late husband, Sir Louis de Bourgh, did his improvements as a young man upon inheritance. Of course it was necessary for more modern comforts to be installed after his death. Mr. Collins will be next to improve Longbourn. I shall have many thoughts for him on the subject."

Mrs. Bennet moved to speak but a warning look from her husband belayed any desire she had to share her indignation at such a notion.

Though the meeting proved a rather mundane affair, it really could not have gone better from the perspectives of the parties involved. Almost everyone behaved unexceptionally; in regards to Lady Catherine, it can be acknowledged that her manners were predictable throughout. Eventually that lady settled the majority of her attention upon Mary, whom she was delighted to confirm played and sang as there was nothing else she liked to recommend more to young ladies than to practice their music. She would have the further felicity of offering Mary the use of one of the pianoforte's at Rosings: the one in the drawing room, it not being feasible to relegate Mrs. Darcy's sister to Mrs. Jenkinson's quarters. Having never heard the lady sing, she knew not what such condescension would cost her.

Mary consistently responded to Lady Catherine's inquiries with proper servility and was deemed to be a practical woman of good sense, exactly what Mr. Collins required in a wife. As she posed question after question, Lady Catherine kept an eye on her nephew and his lady. There was an undeniable bond between the two – never had she seen Darcy so content, not since he was a little boy. She had no objections, only blessings to bestow.

On the carriage ride back to Netherfield, Lady Catherine announced that she would depart first thing the very next morning, "I shall stop in London for a few more days. There is much shopping to do if Anne and I are to travel to Derbyshire in January for your wedding."

Darcy beamed, "I am so glad you will be joining us."

"We shall be spending Christmas with my brother and journey to Pemberley from there, making the trip a bit less burdensome. But I will speak my mind Darcy – a wedding in Derbyshire in the middle of winter is a most inconvenient thing! If I had any idea that you would heed me, I should insist that you wait until the season and marry in London, then Miss Elizabeth might be properly presented, but you are transparently too much in love to wait. And as I intend to persuade the entire family to attend this event, you incommode not only myself and your cousin Anne, who really is not fit for travel in such weather, but all of your relations! Be sure and give Mrs. Reynolds plenty of notice. Pemberley has not been so lively in years!"

"It will be truly wonderful, Aunt."

Chapter 22

Lady Catherine punctually departed Netherfield Hall following an early breakfast. Darcy and Bingley, the only members of the household awake to see her off, looked forward to some leisure time before again repairing to Longbourn for a family dinner, this time in the company of the entire Netherfield party and the Bennet's local relations, Mr. and Mrs. Phillips. As can be expected, Darcy lamented the anticipated awkwardness of such a gathering while Bingley laughed off his concern, perfectly certain that all would be amiable.

"You worry far too much. If the Bennets weathered your aunt's austere presence, surely they will perform admirably this evening. Caroline has been most accommodating of late; certainly, she will be all civility. What have you to fear?"

"Nothing distinct, Bingley. Perhaps my aunt's visit went too smoothly for my comfort. The Phillips are a crude couple; I am assured some discomfort in my interactions with them. You have seen Mr. Phillips in his cups so I need not tell you what is a sorry sight it is. But if Elizabeth can tolerate inquisition from my Aunt, surely I can bear to behold her uncle's complexion."

"Elizabeth is it now?" Bingley laughed as his friend flushed, "Shall we try the sport then?"

"Yes, perhaps we had better. I shall be ready in ten minutes."

Darcy was kept waiting in the hall for Bingley for some time before he finally appeared. Just as they were heading out to the stables, they heard Mrs. Hurst calling from the stairs for her brother to wait. She descended shakily and approached the men with a somber mien, a letter clutched in one outstretched hand.

Mr. Bingley, not always as quick to assess a situation as he should have been, greeted his sister casually, "Good morning Louisa. Late start for you, is it not?"

Mr. Darcy, on the other hand, immediately noticed that Mrs. Hurst was in some degree of distress and silently ushered his companions inside the nearest parlor, moving to shut the door behind the them and provide the siblings with the privacy required.

"Please stay Mr. Darcy," Mrs. Hurst said before he could complete the action, "It is imperative that I speak with both you and my brother." He closed the door behind him but did not proceed farther into the room. Though not knowing what was to come, he was certain his presence was awkward.

Mrs. Hurst turned to Mr. Bingley, "Something dreadful has happened Charles. I know not where to begin!" She sank into the nearest chair and held a handkerchief to her eyes.

Now fully cognizant, Bingley knelt by her side, "Whatever is the matter, my dear sister?"

Darcy stood uncomfortably by while Bingley comforted Louisa and she composed herself. Finally she was able to speak the words needed. As quickly as she could, as if the merest pause would render her mute, she blurted out: "Caroline has disappeared. She has eloped – with Mr. Wickham!"

Bingley started, Darcy paled, and Louisa burst into tears. Again she held forward the letter, still grasped tightly in her hand. Bingley gently took it from her. He walked towards Darcy and read aloud, in a hushed voice:

My dear sister,

I shudder to think of your reaction when you read this, as I can only imagine that you will severely disapprove. For this reason alone I have been forced to be secretive, though my heart has burned to confide in you as of old. Now the deed is done and you shall have no choice but to rejoice in my good fortune.

I depart for Scotland with the man of my dreams, he who is all a man should be. No – he is more than that, far better a man than I ever dared to aspire. What care I for his lack of fortune when I know him to be as gently bred as the very best of our acquaintance? We shall be married forthwith and when next you see me I shall be Mrs. George Wickham. We shall not honeymoon but return to Netherfield as soon as is reasonably possible. I trust Charles will welcome us.

Your loving sister,

Caroline Bingley

"My God! What has she done?" Mr. Bingley exclaimed as he sank into a chair, overcome by the multitude of potential repercussions for such a hasty action on the part of his sister.

"She has provided Wickham with the fortune he always wanted," Darcy replied quietly.

"Do we go after them?"

"She is of age. Her reputation will fare better if they are allowed to proceed uninhibited."

"But what will become of her?" sobbed Louisa. Charles gathered his wits and returned to her side, placing a comforting arm around his eldest sister.

"I shall always receive her, you know that." He looked up at his friend, "He shall be my brother. I cannot let my family become estranged."

Darcy nodded at Bingley in acceptance, made a very correct bow, swiftly exited the room, and walked directly from the house.

He did not spare a thought for what he did or where he went. All he knew was that he needed to be alone – needed time to process this latest development. George Wickham, the man he loathed above any other, was to be his best friend's brother. Worse than that, after marrying Elizabeth, he would be his brother as well, nearly brother to Georgiana too! How was such a thing to be borne?

Darcy's thoughts raced so quickly that, in what seemed like no time at all, he was entering the village of Meryton, happily engaged in its daily rounds of commerce and gossip. Hastily he turned away from the market town and proceeded down the road to Longbourn.

❦

Elizabeth had left early that morning to visit Lucas Lodge in hopes of finding herself alone with Charlotte. Upon arising she had experienced renewed anxiety regarding Lady Catherine's visit, which she had been convinced had gone splendidly the evening before, and only a long talk with her insightful friend would restore her composure. Unfortunately, she found all the family together and was forced to accept their thorough congratulations. Charlotte, perceiving her friend wanted to speak with her, suggested accompanying Elizabeth back to Longbourn under the guise of offering assistance to Mrs. Bennet in her many wedding preparations. They departed together but had only progressed a few steps from the gate when Charlotte, looking behind her, perceived a man walking at a fierce speed towards them.

"Why, surely that is Mr. Darcy hurtling towards us!" she exclaimed.

Elizabeth spun around with an enormous smile that quickly fell when she perceived the disquiet in the approaching form. He only noticed the ladies, having been staring down at the road, when he was nearly upon them and visibly startled by their presence.

"Miss Bennet! Miss Lucas! Please excuse me!"

"Is something wrong Mr. Darcy?" asked Elizabeth with concern, sure her unease had been a premonition of the worst. Had Lady Catherine and her nephew had a falling out because of his engagement? She didn't know if she could bare the guilt of causing a rift in his family and wondered, in fright, "Is he really willing to tolerate one for my sake?"

"Yes. I am afraid there is," replied Mr. Darcy. Struggling to regain his composure, he began pacing two and fro on the spot. Charlotte looked towards her friend to see if she should return home but a subtle gesture bade her to remain. Elizabeth guessed he had more to say and allowed herself to hope it was not what she feared. She knew by now not to try to predict what such behavior on his part indicated. Such endeavors had only caused her needless pain in the past, once when he first declared his affections and again when he proposed. Both ladies waited for Mr. Darcy to provide an explanation.

Eventually recalling himself, Mr. Darcy looked to his patient audience, "You must excuse my discomfiture ladies. Please allow me to bid you both a good morning and express my hope it finds you well."

Both women felt some impatience with his formal pleasantries when something was clearly disturbing him but automatically responded in kind. Reassured by the familiar comfort of the proprieties, he then felt it acceptable to continue, "I have just heard the most inexplicable news. You both know of my efforts to warn the neighborhood of the danger posed by Mr. Wickham's presence, yet it seems I was negligent in protecting the very roof under which I reside. Miss Bingley has most unaccountably eloped with the rascal!"

The ladies' mouths fell agape in a most unbecoming fashion. Fortunately, Mr. Darcy was far too perturbed to notice.

"I cannot understand what possessed her to do such a thing. If nothing else can be said of Caroline Bingley, she has always been status conscious. And now she has put me in the untenable position of marrying the greatest scoundrel it has been my misfortune to know into my very own family!"

Elizabeth's face betrayed an insuppressible grin which lit her countenance to great advantage, catching the attention of her agitated gentleman.

"Is there something in this to amuse you madame?" he asked in exasperation.

"Yes indeed, Mr. Darcy, there is," Elizabeth giggled. He frowned and she hurried to elaborate. "Based on the mad manner in which you are behaving, I feared your aunt had certainly declared herself decidedly against our marriage and had ordered you to bring a halt to the proceedings immediately! Yet instead of such horrible tidings, I receive the pleasure of your referring to our not yet mutual relations as your family." Again she laughed, "Never before have I felt more assured of your devotion, sir! If the idea of Wickham as a relation has not caused you to flea Hertfordshire, Lady Catherine's mere disapproval can prove no obstacle to our happiness."

Darcy paused in his paces before breaking into a tentative smile. Elizabeth always rendered his worries trivial. He should remember in the future not to trouble her with such brooding antics as he had been accustomed to indulge. "Lady Catherine departed Netherfield this morning with every intention of being a wedding guest at Pemberley." They beamed at each other in mutual congratulations for their triumph, but Darcy could not forget Wickham.

"What of Georgiana?" he asked, stepping closer and whispering to her, for once completely unconcerned with the poor manners he was displaying. "How will she handle having to interact with him?" Fortunately Miss Lucas did not feel slighted.

"He shall be a married man, remember? I am sure we can trust his bride to find the means with which to keep him in line."

They smiled in recognition of the formidable wife Miss Bingley would make and Elizabeth deemed it time to bring Charlotte back into the conversation, "It seems we shall have a companion on our walk, which is most fortuitous, as he has just confirmed what I wished to tell you. As you have just heard, all my fears were for naught. Lady Catherine proved a delightful, if commanding lady – all that Mr. Collins claimed her to be. Her graciousness went so far as to approve of me for her illustrious nephew. Can we not be thankful for such affable condescension?"

Charlotte laughed, "Surely one lady could not have torn you two asunder! I have sensed something unique between you from your first dance at the Meryton assembly, long before either of you acknowledged an attachment!"

"You take too much credit Charlotte! Surely you do not wish to deprive my mother of the honor of having first predicted the match?"

"I would indeed, Eliza. I knew you were meant for each other when

I first heard that Mr. Darcy had pronounced Jane the only handsome woman in the room immediately before laying eyes on you! Such contrariness is bound to be thwarted."

The ladies laughed but Mr. Darcy looked embarrassed. "Doubtlessly I was not so very misguided!" he cried. "No, I assure you Miss Lucas, I knew that I had a very special dance partner that night."

Elizabeth blushed and it was Darcy's turn to laugh. The three made their way merrily back to Longbourn, Mr. Wickham and Miss Bingley temporarily behind them.

That evening, when the families gathered for dinner, it was inevitable that Miss Bingley's absence receive comment. As discretely as possible, Mr. Bingley made known to Mr. Bennet the day's events. The older man's eyes grew wide as he listened to the recital. Quickly he glanced towards Darcy and Elizabeth, hoping to ascertain if this recent development had created a rift between the two. Seeing them as enrapt with each other as ever, he was able to respond, "Let me congratulate you then, sir, on your acquirement of what I understand to be a most dashing new brother."

"Dashing perhaps. I only hope, in his quest to cut a good figure, he doesn't bleed Caroline dry."

"Your sister seems to me a strong woman. Surely she can hold her own against him."

"I hope you are correct sir."

Of course, despite the quiet tone of this exchange, news of the elopement soon swarmed through the halls of Longbourn, much to Mrs. Hurst's dismay.

"Oh Mr. Bingley," Kitty cried when she heard. "It is our fault! We completely forgot to say something!"

"What do you mean Kitty," Mr. Bennet demanded. "Please speak clearly."

"When we were shopping in Meryton last week – you remember, do you not Lydia? We saw Miss Bingley escorted by Mr. Wickham on the way into town. They were speaking in a manner that can only be described as intimate."

"Indeed I do remember," concurred Lydia with more enthusiasm than was appropriate, considering the circumstances. "We were so full of shopping that I had entirely forgotten the incident. They did indeed seem to be on quite confidential terms."

"If we had told you what we had seen," Kitty admitted sadly to Mr. Bingley, "you would perhaps have been able to stop them."

"Not so, Miss Kitty," he said in the same soothing voice he had employed with Mrs. Hurst that morning. "I can assure you that it would not have made a bit of difference. Do not blame yourself. Not much can dissuade Caroline once she has set her mind on something. If this is what she wanted, she would have found a way."

"Mr. Bingley is quite right girls," said Mrs. Bennet, who had much more interesting things to discuss than a marriage that did not involve one of her own daughters. She proceeded to orate on the topics in which she was concerned attended by only Mrs. Phillips, who was more than happy to listen once again to all the details of Elizabeth's good fortune, the upcoming ball at Netherfield, and the wedding plans, content that she had heard quite enough of Miss Bingley's exploits to be the first one to share the news with her neighbors in the morning. What a disappointment that the servants managed to spread the word first!

Chapter 23

T he following Sunday Mr. Darcy relocated his place of residence from Netherfield to Longbourn. He was not happy to make the move, despite the unprecedented access to Elizabeth it would allow him, but the idea of being at Netherfield when the newlyweds arrived was by far the more abhorrent option. The elopement was the talk of the town, many an inhabitant of Meryton being happy that the haughty Miss Bingley was the subject of scandal. Mrs. Long took great satisfaction in assuring all who would listen that, Mr. Wickham being a thorough cad, his bride would surely learn to regret such an unfortunate union. Though good wishes such as these abounded in the neighborhood, they did nothing to hinder anticipation for the upcoming ball and following nuptials. Not an invitation for the former was declined; cautiously worded replies were addressed to a woman whom the draftees knew was not currently to be found at home. Mrs. Hurst dutifully opened her sister's mail and assumed command of all the arrangements, despite her ardent desire to flee to London.

Longbourn, particularly by Darcy's standards, was not a large home. Sometimes he wondered if even Pemberley would be large enough to comfortably hold the entire Bennet family. As it was, the noise was sometimes so deafening that Darcy could only compare it to residing in an overflowing inn. The behavior of the family had greatly improved over the months he had known them but that did nothing to alter the fact that they were, by nature, a high spirited clan. Mr. Darcy was often to be found in the library with Mr. Bennet, for whom he had developed an extraordinary sympathy, where the two men read in companionable silence. Though they spoke little, they nevertheless developed a lasting bond in this manner, as is sometimes the way with men. Yet when the time came for Mr. Collins to return to his dear Mary's side, Mr. Darcy readily seized the opportunity to vacate the premises for London, professing the need to collect Georgiana.

Through a series of long and emotional letters, the brother and sister had decided on two things: the first, that it only made sense for Elizabeth and Georgiana to have the opportunity to establish a relationship with each other before marriage made them sisters and, secondly, that George Wickham and his new bride would have to be confronted at some point and it would be better if it did not occur in the middle of the double wedding, to which he and his bride were invited. Also invited to this auspicious event as well as the ball at Netherfield – having gained her brother's permission to attend, as long as she only stood up with either himself or Mr. Bingley – Georgiana had a multitude of incentives to overcome her anxiety at meeting him. A reminder to herself that she was, after all, Miss Darcy of Pemberley and should not shirk from the likes of George Wickham helped to stiffen her spine. But her concerns were not just for her own discomfort. Georgiana, in her unaffected sweetness, could not help but be concerned for the fate of the former Miss Bingley, who had always been unfalteringly kind to her. What would that lady's life be like in the hands of such a man?

So it was that early on the morning of Monday, the 16th of December,

Mr. Darcy departed for London, stopping in Meryton on his way to secure the best rooms the town had to offer for himself and Georgiana to occupy upon his return. He conveniently missed Mr. Collins' arrival by two hours.

Darcy had not stepped a foot inside Netherfield's grounds for an entire week but this did not hinder the friends from meeting daily at Longbourn. Mr. Bingley brought news of the events occurring at the neighboring property while Mrs. Bennet hung on his every word, despite the fact that she usually had already heard it all from Mrs. Hill. Mr. and Mrs. Wickham had returned to Hertfordshire Friday past. On Sunday they made their appearance at church, looking very smug and self-satisfied. Darcy managed to avoid them on this occasion by quickly exiting the building as soon as the service was completed and returning on foot to Longbourn – an exceedingly pleasant exploit as Elizabeth had darted from the church with him. The Wickhams planned to remain at Netherfield until after the wedding, when they would remove to London to spend the season with Mr. and Mrs. Hurst. Wickham had resigned his commission, so lately purchased, and was enjoying spending his new wife's money on properly fitting out his rapidly changing wardrobe. Caroline was very pleased with the figure they cut together and looked greedily forward to hearing her new name announced at all of the year's most elegant balls, where she would relish each instant of her bridal status. The newlyweds seemed to have every intention of becoming permanent fixtures in the Hurst's town home. Louisa was annoyed by their presumption but, as Mr. Hurst looked forward to introducing his dashing new brother at his club, there was little she could do about it.

Georgiana entered Meryton for the first time a week after her brother's departure. They registered at the inn, inspected their room, and left instructions for their belongings before hurrying back into the coach and proceeding to Longbourn. The siblings were giddy in their excitement: Darcy's all pure joy and Georgiana's tinged with nervous anticipation. To him the short ride was interminable but to her it seemed over in an instant. As they approached the house it was in even greater chaos than usual. An elegant coach was being unloaded before the door and all the residents of Longbourn had poured onto the lawn to greet their guests. Georgiana surveyed the many ladies composing the scene before her and wondered which could possibly be Elizabeth. Her eyes were instantly drawn to a statuesque beauty who had spotted the carriage and held one graceful arm aloft, pointing out her find, and looking to an awed Georgiana like every inch a Greek goddess. Suddenly her gaze was grasped by another figure emerging from behind the first, surveying the drive, and bursting into a gleeful gallop as she rushed towards them. Georgiana just had time to smile broadly before her brother stopped the carriage, leaped from the door, and hurried forward to greet Elizabeth.

As they neared each other both slowed to a more dignified pace, suddenly conscious of the many spectators to their unusual behavior. Elizabeth blushed but Darcy could only laugh in contentment, "It is an immeasurable pleasure to see you again Miss Elizabeth." He took her hand and kissed it.

"The pleasure is all mine, sir. I have missed you terribly." Happily they soaked in each other's longed for presence before remembering themselves. They proceeded to the carriage so that Mr. Darcy could help his sister alight and introduce her to her new relations.

"My dear Georgiana, it is my honor to present Miss Elizabeth Bennet. Miss Elizabeth, my sister Georgiana Darcy," he said proudly.

Georgiana was horrified to feel shyness overwhelm her. After all her happy anticipation of this moment, she only managing to squeak out a meek acknowledgment in response to Elizabeth's warm greeting. Too late she wished she had lingered at the inn and rested rather than having rushed forward into the unknown. But Elizabeth read the girl's discomfort, just as she had her brother's when they first met, and smoothed the path ahead. Mr. Bennet also played a part in acclimating Miss Darcy to Longbourn, keeping the remainder of the family from rushing upon the frightened girl by herding them all into the house. His favorite daughter would have all the time she required to perform her magic.

"As you can see we have company, just this moment arrived. My Uncle and Aunt Gardiner join us every Christmas and this year's festivities will be crowned by the added felicity of a ball and a wedding, two actually. You come upon us, Miss Darcy, at a terribly exciting time. Perhaps rather than enter the madhouse, you would first prefer to stroll the grounds so you may stretch your legs? Surely you must want the exercise after spending the whole of the morning in a carriage. Shall I just pop in and grab my bonnet and pelise?"

Mr. Darcy assented and Elizabeth scampered off, leaving the siblings momentarily alone. Darcy looked at his sister with concern, "Are you alright, Georgiana?"

"Yes. It is just that I am utterly disgusted with myself!"

"Georgiana!"

"Why must I be overcome with timidity just when I so want to make a good impression? She is lovely Fitzwilliam. I could not imagine a more perfect wife for you." She hung her head down sadly.

"Just be yourself Georgiana and you and Miss Elizabeth shall be great friends. Of this I am certain."

The reassurance was welcome. When Elizabeth returned and the trio set forth, she made a valiant effort to put Georgiana at ease. In turn, Georgiana did her best to engage in the conversation, a feat that proved far easier than she had feared. Soon all three were comfortably enjoying both the company and the stunning bleakness of the winter vista. As they returned to the house, now appearing as tranquil as it had previously seemed disorderly, Elizabeth commented, "Why, are we not charmingly grouped? Have we not fulfilled the picturesque? Surely we appear to my Aunt Gardiner to uncommon advantage."

An elegant lady had exited the house and was walking forward to meet them. Elizabeth skipped ahead to embrace her. "Forgive me, Aunt, for such a sorry welcome as you have received from me this morning. I should not be disappearing so soon upon your arrival were my guests any others, but these are no ordinary callers." She smiled at Georgiana, who smiled back. "It gives me great pleasure to introduce my companions. Mr. and Miss Darcy, may I present my aunt, Mrs. Gardiner. My dear Aunt, this is Mr. Fitzwilliam Darcy and his sister, Miss Georgiana Darcy."

"It is a pleasure to meet you both. I cannot express how thrilled we are to see our dear Lizzy so very happy."

Darcy was struck. "Could this be Miss Bingley's aunt from Cheapside?" he wondered. "Why, she has an air of complete refinement – can this woman truly be married to Mrs. Bennet's brother?" His reverie was interrupted by Mrs. Bennet herself, who leaned from the doorway and called out that they must come inside and stay for dinner. Mr. Bennet exited the house, shutting his wife in, and extended a less exceptional invitation. Georgiana, much like her aunt, took an instant liking to the sardonic gentleman with the kindly eyes; he helped her to overcome the fear, that she had not yet managed to repress, of actually entering Longbourn itself. Seeing her willingness, Darcy accepted the invitation while buying her some more time to compose herself, pleading the need to return to the inn and dress for dinner. On the ride back they shared their impressions. Georgiana remained somewhat nervous but insisted quite fervently that the lively, eccentric family would most certainly do both Darcys a world of good.

⁂

That evening began Georgiana Darcy's immersion into the Longbourn household. Everyone was on their most subdued behavior in deference to her. Kitty particularly went out of her way to make Miss Darcy comfortable, anxious as she was to please. Inevitably, Lydia asked some bold questions that caused Georgiana momentary discomfort, but overall she had a fine time and looked forward to the next morning's call she had promised to pay. Mrs. Bennet took a motherly interest in Georgiana, keeping her excited matchmaking schemes for the girl safely to herself, and by Christmas she was thoroughly at home at Longbourn. When she entered Netherfield Hall for the first time on the evening of the ball, she felt up to facing even a dozen George Wickhams, ensconced as she was arm-in-arm between Kitty and Lydia, safe and secure amongst her new family.

The house was at its best bedecked for the holiday. Georgiana caught some of Kitty and Lydia's expressive excitement as they passed into the festooned corridor. Mr. Bingley came immediately forward to greet Jane and her parents, who made up the front of the procession of Darcys, Bennets, Gardiners, and a Collins. He turned to introduce them to Mr. Wickham just as Caroline swooped passed them to greet Georgiana with all the warmth of a confidant while patently snubbing Kitty and Lydia. Mr. Darcy frowned and moved forward to intercede when he was confronted by Wickham himself.

"Well Darcy! We meet again at last. I certainly have been looking forward to seeing you ever since I first learned you were in the neighborhood. I had almost taken it into my head that you were intentionally avoiding me."

Darcy grimaced. He could not deny the taunt so chose a safer and more civil topic to pursue. For Bingley, for Georgiana, and especially for Elizabeth, he gathered every drop of his notable self-control and politely said, "Congratulations on your marriage, Wickham."

"Thank you Darcy, thank you! And I understand that you too will soon be depriving society of a most eligible bachelor."

"I have the pleasure of performing that theft. Society will just have to make do without him." Elizabeth had come to Darcy's side and taken his arm. He smiled at her and decided he did not care at all for Wickham – he would not allow himself to be goaded. Relaxing, he said proudly, "Miss Elizabeth Bennet, may I present Mr. George Wickham. Wickham, my intended," and almost casually to his sister, still occupied with Mrs. Wickham, "Georgiana, you remember Mr. Wickham?" Coldly he reintroduced the two as if they had not seen one another since childhood. Georgiana held her head high, despite her discomfiture, while Elizabeth noted how much she resembled her brother the night they met at the Meryton assembly. Wickham quickly returned the Darcys' icy civilities and moved on to greet the Gardiners, Mary, and Mr. Collins – the last of the party to enter. The confrontation was weathered: the worst surely behind them.

Darcy danced with Elizabeth, Georgiana, Jane, and even Kitty, whose performance much surpassed his expectations though she would blush furiously and giggle too much. Elizabeth danced with her uncle, Mr. Bingley, and Mr. Collins (an unfortunate debacle), so when Mr. Wickham approached her for the next set she experienced no pain in refusing, happy as she was to sit with Mr. Darcy for the remainder of the evening.

The Darcy's were charged with depositing Elizabeth and Jane at Longbourn before returning to the inn. On the ride, Mr. Darcy topped off what all agreed to be a memorable evening by enthusiastically regaling his fellow passengers with a most amusing anecdote: "While you were dancing with Mr. Collins, Miss Elizabeth, the new Mrs. Wickham accosted me with the most extraordinary questions. She inquired if, now that marriage would surely do much to heal the breach between Wickham and myself, I would not reconsider giving her husband his due inheritance. At first I was affronted, thinking she referred to a living my father had set aside for him and he rejected, accepting my ample compensation instead. But no, I was mistaken. Mrs. Wickham had much more in mind." Jane, Elizabeth, and Georgiana stared at each other in wonder, the last of these ladies especially surprised by her brother's unfamiliar, mischievous grin.

"She wanted not just a living for her husband, oh no! Not Mrs. Wickham. Somehow she has formed the notion that George Wickham is my – what is the most delicate way to put this – my natural brother!" All three ladies gasped and Darcy laughed at their response, quite impressed with his own sauciness. "To be sure I immediately informed her that her new husband is a precise replica of his father and that my father took a great deal of interest in the lives of all the estate workers."

"You did not!"

"I did."

"Certainly she did not like to think of her husband as a laborer!"

"I would not wish to bare witness to the scene that will surely tran-spire between the newlyweds tonight!" Be assured that all the occu-pants of the carriage enjoyed this mirth excessively, though both Jane and Georgiana would insist that they felt only compassion for the former Miss Bingley.

Chapter 24

Two days later Jane and Mary Bennet were married to Charles Bingley and William Collins, respectively. While Jane's beauty far outstripped her sister's, no one attending would dare be heard to call a bride plain on her wedding day, so all agreed that they had never seen either sister in better looks. Mrs. Bennet was triumphant and Mr. Bennet, some claimed, was seen to be making uncommon use of his handkerchief during the ceremony. A subdued Mr. and Mrs. Wickham stayed close to the Hursts and did not say much to anyone else. Elizabeth, Kitty, and Lydia all attended their sisters while Mr. Darcy stood up with Mr. Bingley, Mr. Phillips performing the honor for Mr. Collins. The day was crisp and clear, no accidents occurred in the kitchen: it was unanimously proclaimed the finest wedding Meryton had seen in many years.

Mr. Darcy, having already invited the Hursts to Pemberley for the wedding, felt it incumbent upon himself to acknowledged the rather subdued Wickhams so far as to extend them that same cordiality at the wedding breakfast. Happily they declined. Both were feeling rather put out by the other and looked forward to the diversions of London where they could indulge their one similarity – a shared desire to cut a dash. Darcy was pleased he would not be in town to witness it.

The Collinses departed the next day for Hunsford – Lady Catherine had been most adamant that her rector must not be absent for yet another Sunday, especially considering that she herself would not be in residence to steer the flock. Mrs. Bennet cried far more than she had expected when she said goodbye, lamenting now that it was too late that she wasn't closer to her third daughter. Mary kissed each relative goodbye with precision, informed her mother that she should not give in to such excessive emotion, joined her new husband in the coach, and left Mrs. Bennet behind her, waving a handkerchief until they were well out of sight.

The following morning there was cause for more emotional good-byes when the Gardiners departed, taking Kitty and Lydia with them. The girls were delighted with the prospect of school in Bath but all pleasures must contain some degree of pain – theirs came in the form of being unable to attend the wedding at Pemberley. It was to their great chagrin that the headmistress odiously insisted they begin a new term, as new pupils, on time. This was bitter indeed. The Gardiners kindly volunteered to take them to London to buy the remainder of their school clothes before Mrs. Gardiner escorted them to Bath. Though the promised shopping did much to soothe their rattled spirits, their departure was still marked by the shedding of a great many tears. Miss Darcy, who joined the family in seeing them off, was particularly touched at the affection shown to her and the many heartfelt declarations of devotion, mainly made by Lydia. It was Kitty, however, who requested that they begin a correspondence, one that was dear to both ladies throughout the remainder of their lives.

Darcy and Georgiana spent the last night of the year quietly at Netherfield, now vacated by the Hursts and Wickhams, before departing for Pemberley the following morning in the company of Mr. Bingley, his new wife, and Elizabeth Bennet.

⁓⁂⁓

As you will undoubtedly observe by the few remaining pages of this text, the following events are rather obvious but I shall, under the assumption that there are those who will be interested, attempt to summarize the details with a modicum of taste and style. Needless to say Jane and Elizabeth were appropriately astonished by the size and scope of Pemberley's house and grounds. "Of all this I am to be mistress!" Elizabeth declared, awed by the thought. Fortunately Mrs. Reynolds was a practical, motherly women and did a great deal to make the future mistress at home. Elizabeth had only a few days with which to acquaint herself with the household before the guests began to appear but, as both Darcys were anxious to aid her in the daunting task, she received ample tutelage. By the time Mr. and Mrs. Bennet arrived, accompanied by Charlotte Lucas, Elizabeth was almost convinced she managed to greet them with at least a semblance of the dignity expected from the future mistress of Pemberley. Mr. Bennet quickly made himself at home in the magnificent library while Mrs. Bennet enjoyed a thorough tour of the house and all its treasures.

The following day brought the arrival of Lady Catherine, Miss De Bourgh, Darcy's uncle, the Earl of _____, and his youngest son, Colonel Fitzwilliam. Elizabeth could tell by their warm manner of greeting what great friends were her betrothed and the Colonel, to whom she took an immediate liking. Warm and friendly as his son was, the Earl was equally imposing. Just as he seemed determined to interrogate Elizabeth with a virtual onslaught of questions, which his sister had not yet managed to answer to his satisfaction, Lady Catherine pointedly interrupted him, "Enough for now brother. It is my turn with the future Mrs. Darcy." The Earl, having a lifetime of experience with his sister, was compliant.

"It is a pleasure to see you again, Lady Catherine," Elizabeth said warmly.

"You may as well call me Aunt Catherine, as I intend to call you Elizabeth. Your sisters' wedding went well I presume?"

"Famously, Aunt Catherine."

"I'm sure your mother will happily provide all the details."

Frequently that evening Darcy and Elizabeth stole furtive glances with each other as they eagerly anticipated the morning. Here were their collected families and friends, getting along far better than either had ever dared to hope, and tomorrow would see them man and wife. For both, it was nothing less than a fabulous dream come true.

❦

Miss Elizabeth Bennet was married to Mr. Fitzwilliam Darcy on a cold but beautiful January morning in the chapel at Pemberley. The bride was dressed simply but the magnificent quality of her gown, complete with Flemish lace, to her mother's infinite satisfaction, added to her beauty a new grandeur. The Darcy family diamonds – presented to her after her arrival at Pemberley, during a tour of her future quarters – adorned her neck and ears. The groom was impeccable in his perfectly tailored coat while the look in his eyes, as he gazed with love at his new wife, promised this to be a union of unusual happiness. Charlotte Lucas, in a new gown for the occasion, attended Elizabeth while Colonel Fitzwilliam, in his dress uniform, stood with Darcy.

Huge quantities of flowers from the greenhouses had been harvested to festoon the seldom used family chapel. The tableau thus created inspired Mrs. Bingley to attempt to render it in embroidery as an anniversary present for her favorite sister.

That same young matron had managed to prevail on her mother not to festoon her head with as many feathers as she deemed appropriate for her daughter's marriage to Mr. Darcy of Pemberley, a very wise move as more lavish headgear would certainly have blocked her daughter's delightful view. Charles whispered, "Will each wedding I attend, now that I am married, affect me so? Or is it just that our own bliss is so recent that makes me unduly sentimental?"

"As long as we remain happy, my love, how can the wedding ceremony not move us? Especially such a magnificent union as this," she quietly responded.

"While I am thrilled to be Darcy's brother, does this not make you, in some respect, my sister as well as my wife?" He barely silenced his mirth at this notion as the couple blushed and beamed at each other, suppressing their urges to laugh.

Georgiana sat next to her uncle and in front of her aunt, both of whom maintained the strictest decorum throughout the ceremony without once hampering her glee. Not that either were in bad spirits – only a few minutes in his nephew's company had convinced the Earl that the match had made him exceptionally happy – but both believed a certain dignity was due to the occasion. Next to Lady Catherine, an unusually animated Anne de Bourgh helped Georgiana to lighten the sobriety their elders had cast over their family's side of the chapel with a smile so broad her face ached, though she did not complain. Several of the upper servants of Pemberley attended the proceedings, sitting behind the family. Mrs. Reynolds took great solace in her handkerchief, which she used to stifle the happy sobs that continuously threatened to emanate: not even Mrs. Bennet was so openly overjoyed. The happy couple planned a tour of the Lakes for their honeymoon but would not leave until late spring. For the time being, they would happily nest at Pemberley excepting only a short spell in London, at Aunt Catherine's insistence.

◦◦◦

The years were good to Mr. and Mrs. Darcy. Their marriage was long, fruitful, and marred only by those tragedies that are inevitable in every life. It was many years before Mr. and Mrs. Collins inherited Longbourn and when the time came Mrs. Bennet remained, not to die for many years after a happy life, virtually devoid of suffering. She and Mary, who also outlived her husband, grew quite close over the years in which they amiably cohabited, finding common ground in the mutual joy they experienced in fretting over Mary's many sons.

Lydia and Kitty both made excellent progress in school and though the former remained a silly, intellectually insubstantial lady throughout her life, she was perfectly happily married to an equally silly but wealthy young man who doted on her and their children. Kitty, on the other hand, grew quite refined and made an unexpected splash on society. She married a handsome and gentlemanly baronet of old family, thereby gaining the precedence Lydia had always professed to want over her elder sisters and would always begrudge Kitty. Lady Stratton threw herself wholeheartedly into the role of patroness to a village, inspired by the example set for her at Pemberley, and spent her life contentedly fulfilling the obligations of wealth while paying little heed to its entitlements.

Needless to say Jane and Bingley were happy. Mr. Bennet's dire predictions that two such kindhearted persons would surely be abused proved false, for Mr. Bingley took a strong hand over the estate he eventually purchased not thirty miles from Pemberley. Only the Wickhams still managed to have the run of him, as they always seemed to be just outside their means and in need of only the smallest assistance to get by, but Charles and Jane were good natured enough not to bear a grudge towards the couple.

Who else can I provide with a happy ending? Why one Charlotte Lucas, who often visited Pemberley and after a few years married Mr. Westover, the rector of the nearby village of Kympton, thereby permanently ensconcing herself in the Darcy's intimate circle. And then, of course, there is Georgiana Darcy. Unfortunately, her tale will have to wait until a muse named Jane once again comes calling.

The End